THE DUKE IS DECEIVED

Suddenly the Duke noticed that the head he could now see under the canopy of the four-poster was the same colour as the sun climbing up the sky outside.

It flashed through his mind that perhaps Mrs. König had left The Abbey and her place in this room had been taken by one of the servants.

But he could never imagine in his wildest dreams anything like that happening at Minster Abbey.

Yet why was this person in bed not Mrs. König?

Instinctively and without even thinking about it, he drew nearer.

Now he saw lying in the bed the most beautiful girl he had ever seen in his whole life.

Her glorious golden hair was falling over her bare shoulders.

Her eyelashes were dark against the pink and white translucence of her skin.

For a moment the Duke thought that he must be dreaming or seeing a vision.

Then he realised that the girl, who seemed so small in such a large bed, was definitely alive and breathing.

THE BARBARA CARTLAND PINK COLLECTION

Titles in this series

1. The Cross Of Love
2. Love In The Highlands
3. Love Finds The Way
4. The Castle Of Love
5. Love Is Triumphant
6. Stars In The Sky
7. The Ship Of Love
8. A Dangerous Disguise
9. Love Became Theirs
10. Love Drives In
11. Sailing To Love
12. The Star Of Love
13. Music Is The Soul Of Love
14. Love In The East
15. Theirs To Eternity
16. A Paradise On Earth
17. Love Wins In Berlin
18. In Search Of Love
19. Love Rescues Rosanna
20. A Heart In Heaven
21. The House Of Happiness
22. Royalty Defeated By Love
23. The White Witch
24. They Sought Love
25. Love Is The Reason For Living
26. They Found Their Way To Heaven
27. Learning To Love
28. Journey To Happiness
29. A Kiss In The Desert
30. The Heart Of Love
31. The Richness Of Love
32. For Ever And Ever
33. An Unexpected Love
34. Saved By An Angel
35. Touching The Stars
36. Seeking Love
37. Journey To Love
38. The Importance Of Love
39. Love By The Lake
40. A Dream Come True
41. The King Without A Heart
42. The Waters Of Love
43. Danger To The Duke
44. A Perfect Way To Heaven
45. Follow Your Heart
46. In Hiding
47. Rivals For Love
48. A Kiss From The Heart
49. Lovers In London
50. This Way To Heaven
51. A Princess Prays
52. Mine For Ever
53. The Earl's Revenge
54. Love At The Tower
55. Ruled By Love
56. Love Came From Heaven
57. Love And Apollo
58. The Keys Of Love
59. A Castle Of Dreams
60. A Battle Of Brains
61. A Change Of Hearts
62. It Is Love
63. The Triumph Of Love
64. Wanted – A Royal Wife
65. A Kiss Of Love
66. To Heaven With Love
67. Pray For Love
68. The Marquis Is Trapped
69. Hide And Seek For Love
70. Hiding From Love
71. A Teacher Of Love
72. Money Or Love
73. The Revelation Is Love
74. The Tree Of Love
75. The Magnificent Marquis
76. The Castle
77. The Gates Of Paradise
78. A Lucky Star
79. A Heaven On Earth
80. The Healing Hand
81. A Virgin Bride
82. The Trail To Love
83. A Royal Love Match
84. A Steeplechase For Love
85. Love At Last
86. Search For A Wife
87. Secret Love
88. A Miracle Of Love
89. Love And The Clans
90. A Shooting Star
91. The Winning Post Is Love
92. They Touched Heaven
93. The Mountain Of Love
94. The Queen Wins
95. Love And The Gods
96. Joined By Love
97. The Duke Is Deceived

THE DUKE IS DECEIVED

BARBARA CARTLAND

Barbaracartland.com Ltd

First published on the internet in October 2012
by Barbaracartland.com Ltd

ISBN 978-1-908411-98-3

The characters and situations in this book are entirely imaginary and bear no relation to any real person or actual happening.

Printed and bound in Great Britain
by Mimeo of Huntingdon, Cambridgeshire.

THE BARBARA CARTLAND PINK COLLECTION

Dame Barbara Cartland is still regarded as the most prolific bestselling author in the history of the world.

In her lifetime she was frequently in the Guinness Book of Records for writing more books than any other living author.

Her most amazing literary feat was to double her output from 10 books a year to over 20 books a year when she was 77 to meet the huge demand.

She went on writing continuously at this rate for 20 years and wrote her very last book at the age of 97, thus completing an incredible 400 books between the ages of 77 and 97.

Her publishers finally could not keep up with this phenomenal output, so at her death in 2000 she left behind an amazing 160 unpublished manuscripts, something that no other author has ever achieved.

Barbara's son, Ian McCorquodale, together with his daughter Iona, felt that it was their sacred duty to publish all these titles for Barbara's millions of admirers all over the world who so love her wonderful romances.

So in 2004 they started publishing the 160 brand new Barbara Cartlands as *The Barbara Cartland Pink Collection*, as Barbara's favourite colour was always pink – and yet more pink!

The Barbara Cartland Pink Collection is published monthly exclusively by Barbaracartland.com and the books are numbered in sequence from 1 to 160.

Enjoy receiving a brand new Barbara Cartland book each month by taking out an annual subscription to the Pink Collection, or purchase the books individually.

The Pink Collection is available from the Barbara Cartland website www.barbaracartland.com via mail order and through all good bookshops.

In addition Ian and Iona are proud to announce that The Barbara Cartland Pink Collection is now available in ebook format as from Valentine's Day 2011.

For more information, please contact us at:

Barbaracartland.com Ltd.
Camfield Place
Hatfield
Hertfordshire AL9 6JE
United Kingdom

Telephone: +44 (0)1707 642629
Fax: +44 (0)1707 663041
Email: info@barbaracartland.com

THE LATE DAME BARBARA CARTLAND

Barbara Cartland who sadly died in May 2000 at the age of nearly 99 was the world's most famous romantic novelist who wrote 723 books in her lifetime with worldwide sales of over 1 billion copies and her books were translated into 36 different languages.

As well as romantic novels, she wrote historical biographies, 6 autobiographies, theatrical plays, books of advice on life, love, vitamins and cookery. She also found time to be a political speaker and television and radio personality.

She wrote her first book at the age of 21 and this was called *Jigsaw*. It became an immediate bestseller and sold 100,000 copies in hardback and was translated into 6 different languages. She wrote continuously throughout her life, writing bestsellers for an astonishing 76 years. Her books have always been immensely popular in the United States, where in 1976 her current books were at numbers 1 & 2 in the B. Dalton bestsellers list, a feat never achieved before or since by any author.

Barbara Cartland became a legend in her own lifetime and will be best remembered for her wonderful romantic novels, so loved by her millions of readers throughout the world.

Her books will always be treasured for their moral message, her pure and innocent heroines, her good looking and dashing heroes and above all her belief that the power of love is more important than anything else in everyone's life.

"When you are in love, the world becomes a different place. The sky is bluer, the moon is brighter, the mountains are more beautiful, the air is clearer and you want to love everybody – and funnily enough everybody wants to love you."

Barbara Cartland

CHAPTER ONE
1875

Prince Johann II of Liechtenstein was busy in his sitting room in the Schloss Vaduz.

The pile of papers in front of him was gradually decreasing and yet, as he gazed forlornly at them with a sigh, he realised that there were still very many of them.

He was still tidying up the mess that had been left, he ruminated, by the German Confederation.

The Monarchy of Liechtenstein was hereditary in the male line only and Johann had succeeded his father as Prince four years earlier.

The Liechtensteiners were intensely proud of their Ruler when so many other countries, like Switzerland, had become Republics.

The Schloss Vaduz looked like a cross between a Medieval fortress and a granary, so the wits joked, but the interior was very different.

The Prince's collection of paintings, to which he was always adding, was priceless and the object of great envy in other Monarchies.

The Schloss Vaduz was enormous and, although his family was small, there were a good number of rooms in use.

And the Schloss was certainly the most luxurious building of the century and the Prince was very proud of it.

He signed his name with a flourish on a particularly bureaucratic letter from the German Chancellor's office.

Then, as he pushed to one side the rest of the papers in the pile, one of his equerries appeared.

Prince Johann looked up, feeling irritated because he disliked being interrupted.

"I apologise for disturbing Your Royal Highness," the equerry said, "but Princess Zelda of Brienz has called to see you."

The Prince looked astonished as the Princess lived in Switzerland with her family, who did not often come to Liechtenstein.

"Show Her Highness in," he ordered and rose from his writing desk.

The equerry bowed and hurried away.

A few moments later he returned and announced,

"Princess Zelda, Your Royal Highness."

Into the sitting room came an extremely attractive, in fact very beautiful young woman.

The Prince had not seen her for nearly two years and now he reckoned that she must be nearly twenty.

She had become a great beauty, as her mother had been. Her heart-shaped face and clear complexion made her outstandingly attractive and her long golden hair was more likely to belong to an angel from Heaven.

She stood for a moment in the doorway, looking to make sure it was him and then she ran towards the Prince.

"I thought that you would be surprised to see me, Cousin Johann," she began. "But I need your help and it is far too long since I last saw you."

"Just what I was thinking myself," he replied to her. "You are now even prettier, dear Zelda, than you were that Christmas when you fascinated everyone in the country."

"Now you are flattering me. But I enjoy that and now I have come to ask for your help. You are the one person I would trust to give me the right answer."

The Prince smiled.

"In other words the answer you want yourself!"

"Exactly," Zelda replied.

"Well, first we must have a glass of wine," he said. "As you must be tired after your long journey, I suggest you take off your hat and cape."

As she stood in front of him, he thought that her figure was just as perfect as her complexion and she was undoubtedly one of the most beautiful young women he had seen for a long time.

As if he knew what to do, a servant came hurrying in with a bottle of the best Liechtenstein wine.

The Princess, having accepted a glass, sat down on the sofa and the Prince sat in a chair near her.

As the door closed behind the servant, he enquired,

"Now what has happened? What is the trouble?"

"Need you ask?" Zelda exclaimed. "Papa is trying to marry me off to another Ruler. This time he comes from the Balkans and is even more unpleasant than the last one he chose for me!"

The Prince knew his cousin was determined that his precious only child should marry at the very least a ruling Prince and produce a large family.

And it would make his position in Switzerland even more influential than it was already.

In 1848 Switzerland had received a completely new constitution, but it was still a Republican country without a Royal Ruler and had in the last several years enjoyed an exceptional political stability with its mixture of Canton and Federal Governments.

But the older families who had always supported their Royalty were, as Prince Johann knew, determined to be respected and venerated as they had been in the past.

His cousin, Zelda's father, however, had suffered a severe blow when he was a young man.

He had been the victim of an avalanche that had crippled him and the doctors had pronounced that it would be impossible for him ever to be the father of children.

He had very recently married an extremely pretty woman – Princess Lois, and it seemed such a tragedy that the two young people could not complete their happiness by bringing a child into the world.

Then unexpectedly, when Princess Lois was thirty, by what appeared to the people around them as a miracle, she produced a daughter as beautiful as herself.

Prince Johann thought that he would never forget the excitement in the family and the emotional celebrations that took place at the Christening.

It seemed as if Zelda had brought light and laughter to her parents.

As she grew up and became as stunningly beautiful as her lovely mother, it was obvious that her father was determined she should make a grand marriage, if possible to a reigning King.

And there were quite a number of them available.

Although they lived quite a distance apart, Prince Johann was well aware of his cousin's ambition and he was not really surprised that Zelda should turn to him for help.

"Now tell me exactly," he said, "what your father is doing to force you into marriage even though you don't like any of the potential bridegrooms."

"'Like' is too mild a word for those who have been produced so far," Zelda replied. "The last one was twenty years older than me and had nothing to talk about except his horses, which I gather are not that well-bred. I suspect the same might be said of their owner!"

Prince Johann laughed.

"That's certainly a very scathing condemnation," he remarked. "But I can understand your father's anxiety. You know as well as I do that our family has always been respected in Switzerland as well as here in Liechtenstein."

"I have heard that you are doing brilliantly, Cousin Johann, but then you are really Royalty, whilst we have nothing to commend us except a large house and an estate that cannot be called a Kingdom under any circumstances."

"But that is how your father likes to think of it."

He paused before he went on slowly,

"I suppose he is thinking that if you produce several sons one of the younger ones could then inherit your Swiss estate, while the eldest would obviously follow his father onto his non-existent throne."

Zelda held up her hands.

"You are going much too fast, Cousin Johann," she protested. "How can you possibly talk about my having all that number of children when I have not yet found a man I could tolerate for two minutes as my husband?"

"I cannot believe that you are as difficult to please as that, Zelda. After all there are handsome and attractive men in every part of the world. Although I admit they are not always Royal."

"Papa has insisted on a grand marriage. It was after I had seen the last unbelievable horror from the Balkans that I ran away."

"So you have run away," Prince Johann exclaimed, "and what am I supposed to do about it?"

"I will tell you exactly what I want," Zelda replied. "I want to go to England."

"To England! But *why*? It's a country your father has shown no interest in and has never even been there."

"You know the answer to that as well as I do."

The Prince stared at her.

"What exactly do you mean by that?" he asked after a moment's silence.

"Do you really think," she asked, "that I could have remained ignorant for ever over what happened?"

There was silence before the Prince asked,

"Who told you the tale you must be referring to?"

Princess Zelda laughed.

"I think it must have been whispered over me in the cradle. By the time I could think for myself, I could see almost everyone who came to our house looking at me in an enquiring manner and whispering to one another that I definitely resembled the Earl."

Prince Johann sat upright in his chair.

"Are you telling me," he asked, "that you believe that fantastic story?"

"Of course I believe it," Zelda flashed back. "You know just as well as I do that everyone in Switzerland and doubtless in Liechtenstein too knows it is the truth."

The Prince gave a deep sigh.

For a moment he could not think of anything to say, as he had never imagined that the rumour about her birth would have reached her tender ears – or, if she had heard it, she would take it seriously.

Of course people were astonished when after nearly ten years of marriage, Princess Lois had become pregnant and given birth to a baby daughter.

It was only the close members of the family who suspected that the Earl of Milver, an extremely handsome Englishman, who had been staying at Brienz nine months earlier, had been infatuated by the lovely Princess Lois.

The doctors had been completely certain that his cousin could never father a child.

Therefore naturally Prince Johann, like the rest of the family, had been astonished when the baby was born.

However, he had determinedly pooh-poohed any suggestions made to him about the Earl of Milver.

When he had met the Earl later in Paris, he realised how good-looking he was and he could easily understand that everywhere he went he would be gossiped about and undoubtedly pursued by endless beautiful women.

There was no doubt as the years passed that the rumour had spread and refused to be suppressed.

It was all the more plausible when Zelda showed so many characteristics that were definitely English.

Her pink and white complexion for one thing was a characteristic everyone recognised as being English.

So was her fair hair – it was the colour of the sun rising over the mountains in the morning.

She was also extremely intelligent. In fact so much so that it was one of the first attributes that people found strange and her father and mother, charming though they were, were not notable for their brains.

The Earl of Milver had, as far as Prince Johann was aware, never returned to Switzerland.

He later became the fourth Duke of Milverden, but was killed in a riding accident when he was still unmarried.

The Dukedom had gone to a cousin who, Prince Johann calculated, must be around twenty-seven or twenty-eight by now.

He had not met him and as far as he was concerned, he had no wish to discuss the Milverdens whether of the present or the past.

Yet now, to his astonishment, Princess Zelda was saying that she wished to go to England.

Choosing his words carefully, the Prince declared,

"I suppose, if you do have a great ambition to visit England, it would be possible. But I see no reason for you to do so."

"I have every reason," she replied. "After all, if the late Duke was my father, I have a right to see what the rest of the family are like."

The Prince said nothing and she went on,

"I feel certain they must be superior to the ghastly creatures my father wishes me to marry simply because they have a crown or a coronet on their heads."

"And what good will it do? If you find the Duke is as unpleasant as those whom your father favours, will you come back and accept one of the suitors who has laid his heart at your feet?"

Princess Zelda laughed.

"There is nothing like that about it. They behave as if they are doing me a great favour and are then absolutely astonished when I refuse them!"

Prince Johann's eyes twinkled.

"I just cannot believe that's true. At the same time, because I have always been so fond of you since you were a baby, I would very much like you to marry a man you love and who loves you."

"That is just what I really want. Can you imagine anything worse than being shut up in one of those dreadful small Kingdoms with a number of people with scarcely a brain between any of them and having nothing to do but open Flower Shows or present prizes?"

"What do you want to do?" he asked quizzically.

"For one thing I want to see the world. For another and of course more important, to be sure of my ancestry."

"I cannot imagine how you have been allowed to talk about what the family found astonishing at the time, but brought them great happiness. Although there was a certain amount of gossip it has, I think, been forgotten as the years passed."

Princess Zelda chuckled.

"Don't believe it! I hear people whispering when I enter a ballroom. If I go within hearing distance of what they are saying, they are talking about the Earl, as he was then, and how remarkable and amazing it was that I was born nine months after he left Switzerland."

The Prince thought there was no point in arguing and he therefore remarked,

"So you want to meet the present Duke and tell him that he is your relation?"

"I expect he knows that already and, as you will readily appreciate, bad news travels much faster than good. Even in far-away England they must find a story like this intriguing."

"So what do you want me to do, Zelda?"

"I want you to arrange for me to go to England and be received by Queen Victoria. After that I will be able to have a look round and meet a good many Englishmen."

"If you are thinking of marrying English Royalty, I assure you that the Prince of Wales is very occupied from everything I hear and is in fact married already."

"I am well aware of that, Cousin Johann. His love affairs are so numerous no one can remember them all!"

She laughed before she added,

"I expect you know how badly he behaved in Paris. His latest mistress, I am told, is one of the most beautiful women London has ever seen."

"I cannot think where you have heard this gossip, Zelda. It is absolutely wrong that a girl of your age should know so much."

Zelda laughed.

"I am getting on for twenty and, if I am ever to be free to enjoy my life, the more I know about the gossip in other countries as well as my own, the more it will help in whatever the future holds for me."

Then is a different tone of voice, she pleaded,

"Please, please, Cousin Johann, help me. You do see that if Papa gets his way and I am stuck with some incredibly boring Prince in some unimportant little country where there is nothing to do and nothing to talk about, I think I will go mad."

"I have always been told you are very intelligent, Zelda. But you must realise that is usually a woman's life, especially a Royal woman, whether she likes it or not."

"Of course I realise it. I am determined, if I have to marry, it will be to someone who wants to change things and perhaps make his country, if he has one, great."

The Prince smiled.

"That is exactly what I want you to say, Zelda. The difficulty is to find where such a place exists."

"I cannot tell you how deadly dull my prospective suitors are. Papa has dug them all out from the Balkans, from Germany and even Spain. But none of them seem to have any ambition or any desire to do anything for the world or for that matter for themselves. They are just so pleased to be Royal and to them that's all that's needed."

The Prince laughed because he could not help it.

"It's a sad, sad story," he said. "One could almost call it, '*The Tale of a Girl who did not want to be Queen*'!"

"Now you are laughing at me, Cousin Johann. Do not forget I have to marry the man, I have to tell him he is wonderful and I have to live a life of complete and utter boredom. If their fathers are as boring as the Princes I have met so far, my children will be utterly boring too!"

The Prince coughed discreetly and she continued,

"Now you can understand why I want to see what my real father looked like. I could hardly say that to my mother or to Papa whose name I bear."

"Of course you would not do anything so unkind," the Prince countered sharply.

"That is why I have come to you. Help me to go to England," she begged. "Perhaps if I am disappointed with the Duke, I will realise I am a changeling and accept the next man Papa produces for me."

"Very well, Zelda. You can have your own way. But you have to promise me that if you are disillusioned, as I think you may be in England, you will come back and think twice before you throw over the next proposal of marriage."

Zelda gave a little cry.

"Do you really mean it? Oh, Cousin Johann, I knew you would help me! Now I am really excited. I have a feeling, although I may well be wrong, that I will find something very different in England from all I have found so far."

"I am sure all our neighbours have been delighted to welcome you, but England is different. Although I have a number of friends who are English, I have often thought it difficult to make any comparison between them and my friends from Switzerland and other countries around us."

"That is exactly what I want to find out. Now I am here, and Papa thinks I am staying with you, how soon can I leave?"

The Prince held up his hands.

"Now you are bullying me. I think really I should consult your father first before I send you off on this wild goose chase."

"You would not be so unkind as to give me away," Zelda frowned. "When I reach England, I may find it is so disillusioning that I will come back at once. In which case there would be no need for you to upset Papa."

"Do you think it will perturb your father that you are going to England without telling him?"

Zelda thought for a moment and then she said,

"I think it may. He has always behaved strangely if ever anyone speaks of England and invariably changes the subject."

The Prince could understand this and then he asked,

"Does your mother talk about it?"

Zelda shook her head.

"No, Mama is as silent as Papa. That is what made me convinced from the very beginning that the story is true and I *am* the daughter of the fourth Duke of Milverden."

Almost instinctively Prince Johann looked over his shoulder as if he was afraid someone might be listening.

"You really must not say such things, at any rate not outside this room."

"I promise you I will be very discreet. I just want to go to London, meet Queen Victoria and somehow get introduced to the present Duke without, if at all possible, his knowing who I am or why I have come."

The Prince looked surprised.

"I thought you were going to rush in with flags flying and tell him at once that you are his relation."

"I have a distinct feeling he would not particularly appreciate that. I have always believed that the English, who are proud of their status, hush up any gossip that is not favourable and behave as if it had never happened."

Prince Johann laughed.

"That is more or less true. I assure you that they will expect you to be sweet, gentle and very discreet."

"I will try my best, but it does not exactly sound like me!"

"Well, remember, just as you judge the Englishmen you meet, so they will judge you as a representative of Switzerland. You must therefore behave as they expect you to."

"Which, as far as I can make out now, is to be exceedingly dull," Zelda retorted.

"I am sure that you are much too intelligent and far too clever to cause a scandal. But while you are away I will be keeping my fingers crossed."

Zelda laughed and jumped up from the sofa.

"I just knew you would help me, Cousin Johann. Thank you for being just so understanding and so different from the men I have met recently."

"Forget them, Zelda. After all there are plenty of suitable men here and in other countries. You don't have to marry someone boring from the Balkans."

"I wish Papa could hear you say that. He has been droning on and on at me morning, noon and night. It was only today, when he went to the other end of the estate and will not be back for several nights, that I decided I had had enough and came at once to you."

"I am always delighted to see you, Zelda. Now, as you expect me to do, I must set the ball rolling. First of all, and this is important, you cannot go to England without a chaperone."

"Of course I realise that," the Princess replied to his surprise. "I have had it drummed into me ever since I was seventeen which is now three years ago – 'a lady, wherever she goes, must have a chaperone.'

'A lady must not get herself talked about as being fast or improper.'

'A lady must know little and say little,' and all that goes for most of the women I meet at home!"

The Prince laughed because he could not help it.

And then he quizzed her,

"Who is the chaperone who has brought you here?"

"My old Governess and, as she is the widow of one of our late lamented Statesmen, she is exactly the sort of chaperone both you and Papa would expect me to have."

"I look forward to meeting her."

"She is seeing a friend who lives nearby, but will join us this evening for dinner if that is all right for you."

Zelda looked at him with her large blue eyes before she added,

"I was hoping it might be possible to leave early tomorrow morning – "

"In which case we will have to make it possible. Have you an entourage?"

"My lady's maid, who was actually my nanny at one time, and is discretion itself, will tell you even more forcefully than I can how ghastly the men are that Papa wants me to marry."

"Forget them," the Prince advised her again, "and I have a feeling that you have worked yourself up against the

Swiss and all the Balkans to the point that whatever they did or said you would either dislike or ignore it. Therefore we must see if a change of climate will bring you a change of heart."

"That sounds good sense to me," Zelda replied. "At the same time, if I come back married to a crossing-sweeper because he is English and handsome, do not be surprised!"

"The person who will be surprised is your father," the Prince countered, "and I can assure you I will refuse to take any blame for having led you astray – "

Zelda kissed his cheek.

"I love you, Cousin Johann, and I will not get you into more trouble with Papa than I can help. I know you are the only one who could help me, the only relative who can understand my problems."

She paused for a moment,

"I am not surprised that the people here love you and find that you are a perfect Ruler."

The Prince chuckled.

"Now you are merely flattering me to get your own way, which you have already succeeded in doing. But I am glad you appreciate that I am now actually being called by the people of Liechtenstein, *Johann the Good*."

"Yes, I have heard that and I am sure that it's true. Even my Papa, who will never praise anyone, except some horrible man he wants me to marry, tells me that you are a benefactor of the poor as well as a Patron of the Arts."

"Now you are flattering me again, simply because you have gained your own way, Zelda, and I am not going to listen. But I would suggest I make arrangements for you to leave for England first thing tomorrow morning."

He saw her draw in her breath with excitement,

"Otherwise your father may turn up unexpectedly and forbid you to leave Europe. Then there will be nothing we can do but send you to the Balkans."

"You would never be so cruel! But you are quite right, the quicker I go away the safer it will be. So please, please, darling Cousin Johann, set all the arrangements in motion as you promised you would."

"I will do it immediately. Now come and look at the new picture I bought last week. I think it is one of the best in my whole collection."

"I would love to see it," Zelda answered, slipping her arm through his. "I know that your taste is impeccable, which is how I try to make mine."

They left the room and, as they walked down the passage, the Prince was wondering whether he was indeed making a great mistake in allowing this impulsive and very lovely young woman make what the family would consider a highly improper journey to England.

Then he felt sure that, if she was to be under the protection of Queen Victoria, who everyone respected so much, she would not come to any harm.

'It's only fair,' he thought to himself, 'that Zelda should have a look round before she is married off to some obscure Principality in Germany or the Balkans where, as she said herself, she will be exceedingly bored.'

Zelda looked up at him and he had the idea that she was reading his thoughts.

"Give me a chance, Cousin Johann," she pleaded, "to spread my wings and see a different world from the one I have seen before. Up to now I have only been able to travel in my mind. Now, as I set out for England, I have a feeling it will be very unlike anything I have dreamt of."

"There will certainly not be so many mountains or so much snow."

"Now you are teasing me. You know as well as I do that what I want to see are different men. Unless what I have read has been completely untrue, they will be much more intelligent, much better-looking and much more fun than those I have encountered so far."

Prince Johann had a distinct feeling that this idea might prove dangerous.

Then he told himself that he was worried because his cousin was so beautiful.

'She has the sort of loveliness that will attract men wherever she goes or whatever she might do,' he decided. 'She also has a great deal of commonsense and that in my opinion is more important than anything else.'

They had now reached the end of the passage.

He opened the door into his secretary's room, who would make all the necessary arrangements for her.

And, as he did so, he had a strange feeling he was releasing this exquisite little creature beside him into a new and potentially dangerous world.

*

It was later on that evening when they were having dinner that Frau Horwitz, who was to be Princess Zelda's chaperone, piped up,

"I have not been to England for many years, but I have heard that Queen Victoria has done marvels since she came to the throne. England has more power as a country than it has ever enjoyed before."

"That is certainly true," the Prince agreed. "It is amazing all that she has managed to achieve."

"Her uncle and some of her other relations had a very bad name for their flirtatious behaviour," she added. "So I can understand that Her Majesty the Queen is very upset at the way her son behaves."

"I don't suppose he is as bad as all that," Prince Johann remarked. "After all he is handsome and has, I am told, great charm. It's not surprising that women run after him."

"He has a very good wife," Frau Horwitz retorted.

The Prince thought that might apply to a number of people and it was hardly fair to criticise the poor Prince of Wales who, he was told, was not allowed by his mother to take part in any of the Affairs of State.

He thought, however, it was a mistake to discuss the Prince of Wales and his love affairs in front of Zelda.

So he changed the subject and spoke about all the innovations he had recently introduced into Liechtenstein.

He spoke too of his extensive art collection that was growing larger year by year.

"You are quite right," Zelda said to him later in the evening when they were alone together, "not to let my old Governess think I am interested in meeting the Prince of Wales. She is shocked at his behaviour and is determined to keep me from meeting him whilst I am in London."

"I think you are quite safe. From all I have heard of Prince Edward, he much prefers older married women and his name is never coupled with anyone as young as you."

"That's a pity," Zelda sighed, "because I would like to meet him. I feel we would have much to talk about."

"Now listen to me," the Prince asserted. "If you are going to travel to England, you must not get yourself a bad reputation, which will undoubtedly be carried back here and to your father in Switzerland."

Zelda grinned.

"Now you are trying to scare me. I told you I want to meet the Duke because I am sure he is my relation and just to have a look at Englishmen as a whole. After all, if I am half English, I should have some affinity with them."

With difficulty the Prince prevented himself from looking over his shoulder to see if anyone was listening.

"I beg of you to be careful," he urged her. "I had no idea that you had been told the story of your birth and the least other people know of it the better."

"Of course I would not talk to anyone but you and perhaps the Duke when I meet him," Zelda replied. "But you must see, Cousin Johann, that, if I am half English, I want to see which half belongs where!"

She breathed in deeply and then added quietly,

"I have a feeling that England will be very different in reality from all I have read about it in books."

"I can understand your curiosity, Zelda, but at the same time please be discreet. Remember that what might have occurred twenty years ago should have been forgotten by this time. I expect no one in England was aware of it then or indeed is so now."

"That in a way makes it more intriguing," Zelda said. "If I say to the present Duke, 'I am your relation', do you think he will give a cry of horror and hurry away in case he is contaminated by me?"

"If he is a gentleman, he will do neither of those things, but I do beg of you to meet him in quite an ordinary way. I am sure when you do so, you will think it a mistake to bring up past events and old scandals."

"I think it is something I should be very proud of," Zelda persisted.

He did not reply and after a moment she went on,

"You can hardly blame my Mama for wanting love even if it was illegitimate. Although we have never talked about it, I know she wants me to marry someone I love and to have quite a number of children."

"Of course she wants that for you. It is what every woman wants."

The Prince was aware that Zelda had been talking dreamily. It was as though she had been telling him of her private thoughts and feelings that to her were very real.

Gazing at her in the candlelight from the chandelier in the drawing room, he thought that she was undoubtedly one of the most ethereal young women he had ever seen.

Although he had no intention of saying so aloud, it was undoubtedly her English blood that gave her such a wonderful skin and the pale beauty of her fair hair.

'Perhaps she will be a huge sensation in London,' he mused. 'That would certainly stop her from worrying about the Duke, whatever he may be like.'

It suddenly occurred to him that he had hardly heard of the present Duke at all.

Sometimes he read the English newspapers, but he could not recall his name being mentioned and this seemed rather strange because he knew that a Duke in England was the most important and influential of all the grandees.

A Duke should be in attendance on Queen Victoria at Windsor Castle and would therefore be mentioned in *The Court Circular.*

The Prince, however, rarely bothered to read that part of the newspaper.

But a great many Englishmen visited Liechtenstein regularly and none of them who had stayed with him at the Schloss mentioned his name in their conversation.

'Perhaps,' he thought to himself, 'he is a constant traveller or he prefers the North of England. In which case Zelda will be disappointed if she does not meet him.'

That, he murmured to himself finally, would be a much more convenient end to the story and to the scandal than anything Zelda could contrive.

CHAPTER TWO

When Prince Johann really put his heart into doing something, he did it well.

Zelda mused that she had never known anyone take more trouble or be more aware of the small difficulties of travel that others would either have forgotten or ignored.

The first question the Prince asked her was,

"Where are you going to stay in London?"

Zelda smiled at him.

"I have not thought about it, but I presume we can go to a hotel."

"It would be much better not to, Zelda. People are always complaining hotels are full. But what they really find is that they are overcrowded and there are difficulties and discomforts they do not have at home."

"Where do you suggest I go?" Zelda asked him.

The Prince thought for some minutes.

"I think it would be wise if you went to one of my old friends who has a large house just outside Mayfair in Belgrave Square. She is getting on for seventy now, but she used to come and stay here frequently years ago when you were too small to remember her."

"Then, of course, if she is a friend of yours, Cousin Johann, I would be delighted to meet her."

She gave him a provocative glance and added,

"I suspect that you were either in love with her or she was in love with you!"

"That is something a well brought up young girl does not say to anyone," the Prince propounded firmly.

Zelda giggled.

"I know that, but, because you have always been so kind and sweet to me, you are different. I feel I can say to you all the things I ought to be able to say to my father, but unfortunately he would not understand."

"I think he would be shocked at most of them."

Zelda nodded.

"Of course he would. That is why I am quite sure that the man I call Papa is not really my father."

"I can only say to you a thousand times," the Prince reiterated, "that those are things you should not say and you must never repeat them outside this room."

He spoke rather sternly, but Zelda jumped up, put her arms round his neck and kissed his cheek.

"I love you, Cousin Johann," she said, "and while the world outside calls you *Johann the Good*,' I will call you *Johann the Marvellous*, entirely because you are so wonderful to me."

The Prince could not help reflecting that it would take a exceedingly clever man to handle this adorable but most unpredictable young beauty.

"Now sit down quietly," he suggested, "and stop shocking me, while we think out your journey to England."

He thought that she was about to argue with him and he went on quickly,

"Otherwise your father will arrive to put a stop to all this."

Zelda gave a little cry.

"Of course he will. Oh, please, please, my dearest Cousin Johann, hurry and get me out of the way."

"That is just what I am trying to do. I was telling you about my dear friend. Her name is Lady Craven and, as I have already told you, she owns a house in Belgrave Square. I believe that now she finds it difficult to move about, so she will surely be in London when you arrive."

"And she will not mind having me to stay?"

"I think she will be delighted and you will find she knows more about the *Beau Monde* than anyone else in London and she will undoubtedly tell you all you want to know about the fascinating Social world."

"There is only one Social person I want to meet," Zelda insisted, speaking more to herself than to the Prince.

"I know that, but it would be a mistake to rush into London asking everyone where he is. For all I know he may be married by now."

"Of course he may, but I still want to see him and naturally through him as many of the Milvers as I can, who are my family, as I think of them."

"You may think it, but not speak it," Prince Johann admonished her. "I am sure you will learn in London that the walls have ears."

"I am not going to let you frighten me now that you have been kind enough to say you will arrange my visit," Zelda said. "It is the most enthralling thing that has ever happened to me and whatever transpires I am determined to enjoy every moment of it."

"That is just what I want you to do, Zelda. Equally you must behave yourself and remember that people expect a girl of your age to be demure and obedient."

"As I am neither, I know I ought to stay at home. But instead, since you have opened 'the path to the moon,' I would be very stupid if I did not take it."

The Prince smiled benignly at her.

"Now let's get down to work," he insisted. "You will stay with Lady Craven and I will send her a letter by courier so that she will have time to make arrangements for you before you arrive."

Zelda was listening intently and the Prince went on,

"I think in these circumstances it would be a major mistake for you to take Frau Horwitz with you. I will send you with an experienced and respected Courier, who I have used on many occasions. Lady Craven will chaperone you when you arrive in London."

"My Governess will be disappointed. So I think it would be kind, as she has friends in London, if I take her as far as that."

"That's a good idea," the Prince approved. "I don't want to spoil the time you will spend with Lady Craven by having another woman there who would make her feel she could not be as frank as if you were alone together."

"I am the one who is most likely to be frank," Zelda pointed out. "But naturally you are right, Cousin Johann. I will do exactly what you want me to do."

"I hope you will remember those words," the Prince smiled. "But be very careful what you say and whom you make your confidante."

"In fact what you are telling me," Zelda said, "is that I am not to talk to anyone else about the late Duke of Milverden, who I believe was my father."

"You are not even to say that to me," the Prince replied, pointing a finger at her. "Now let me be in touch with my Courier and my secretary to book you seats from here to London and the sooner you leave the better."

"I promise you that Papa will not be aware of my absence until either late tomorrow or the day after that."

"We are taking no risks," he answered. "Unless I am being over-optimistic, Zelda, you will be on your way tomorrow morning."

She clapped her hands with delight.

The Prince left the room, going, she knew, to talk to his secretary who would make all her arrangements.

Zelda went to the window and stood looking out at the beautiful view.

The Schloss Vaduz had been built high up on the side of a hill. There was a valley below and beyond it rose tall mountains and there was still snow on the very top.

Now the sun was shining brightly and it glittered entrancingly. It had a spiritual look about it like that of the halo over an angel's head.

It was a very familiar scene to Zelda, but it never failed to make her feel that she was peeping into another world, a world that could only be reached by her prayers.

'Help me, God,' she prayed. 'Help me not only to find the family I belong to but to find a man who will love me for myself and who I will love for himself.'

She thought of the Princes her father had produced for her and felt a little shudder course through her.

It was not only because they repelled her but also because they were making use of her. Not as a woman, but because of the proud name she bore and also the fact that her father was very rich.

'What I want,' she told the glittering snow, 'is the real love that I believe exists beyond the horizon and of which I spy just a glimmer when I gaze at you.'

Zelda heard the door open and she turned round to see that the Prince had returned.

"Everything has been arranged," he told her. "Now we can enjoy ourselves without worrying."

Zelda ran towards him.

"You are marvellous! I know that you will be kind enough not to tell my Governess that I no longer need her when we reach London. She will not contact her friends until she is sure I no longer have any need of her."

The Prince smiled.

"I will leave her to you, Zelda, but I do beg of you to be careful what you say in her presence. Remember that you are a very precious person to a great number of people. Therefore they are bound to talk about you and that can be dangerous."

"I do realise that, Cousin Johann, and I will be very very careful. I am so grateful to you. It is such a relief to be away from Papa and his prospective bridegrooms."

"Forget them! I have some new pictures to show you that I know you will enjoy. I have also bought several unique books. Although they were amazingly expensive, they will enhance the reputation of my library."

"Which is already fantastic, but please show me the pictures first. You know that I have always admired your paintings since I was a small child."

They went into the picture gallery.

As the Prince was very knowledgeable about art, Zelda found herself entranced. He had some *objects d'art* that he had bought in Paris and other parts of Europe that Zelda had never seen.

They were both quite surprised when they realised how much time they had spent there and it was now getting late in the afternoon.

Zelda was fortunate enough to have dinner alone with the Prince after she had changed into a pretty evening gown, and Frau Horwitz was dining with her friend.

Zelda was thrilled to have her cousin all to herself.

While the servants were in the room, they talked about pictures and other subjects that interested them both.

It was only when they were alone in the blue sitting room that the Prince had made particularly his own that Zelda talked about herself.

"It has been wonderful having dinner with you," she began, "and having a really interesting conversation. I cannot tell you how boring the meals are at home with far too many people in attendance on Papa and they never say anything that is not extremely uninteresting."

"You must try not to be too critical of ordinary people, Zelda. You will find that most of them either talk about themselves or their own interests. You have to listen and pretend you are riveted even if you are not."

"Now once again you are telling me how to behave like a woman. I am certain that is what all men expect, except of course the man I am looking for."

"Suppose you never find him?"

"Then I will come back here I suppose and in sheer desperation marry one of those tiresome idiotic Kings or Princes that Papa has found for me."

Zelda spoke so bitterly that the Prince laughed.

"Now you are being over-dramatic. You know as well as I do that, if you had a Kingdom at your feet, you would change everything overnight and make a success of it even if all your subjects were determined you should do nothing of the kind."

"You are assuming too much, Cousin Johann. I am woman enough to want a man to help me. And then I am prepared to make him believe it is me who is helping him."

The Prince chortled.

"That's the right attitude. I am certain that, if you stay with me long enough, I will soon teach you how to be the perfect wife."

"In which case you will have to find me the perfect husband. I can assure you that they don't grow at home on gooseberry bushes!"

They laughed and talked on until it was time to go to bed.

Then the Prince told her,

"The carriage will be waiting at the front door at eight o'clock tomorrow morning. You have to catch a train that leaves early to carry you through the first part of your journey. There will only be one change for you to make before you reach Ostend. That will cause no difficulty as the Courier has undertaken the journey a thousand times."

Zelda put her arms round his neck.

"Oh, thank you, thank you, Cousin Johann! I will never forget how kind you have been to me. If things go right, which I know you doubt, it will all be due to you."

"I now have a feeling that all will be well," he said. "But you may have rather more difficulty than you expect in eventually achieving your goal."

"I am sure you will pray for me, as I will be praying for myself. I just cannot believe we will not win."

She kissed him and then went to her bedroom.

Because she was excited at what was happening, it took her a little time to go to sleep.

When she did, she dreamt that she was climbing up the side of a mountain and the sun at the top was glittering, as if it was encircled with a halo of light.

*

She set off the next morning with Frau Horwitz curtsying respectfully to Prince Johann.

Zelda kissed him on both cheeks and he held her close in his arms.

"Now take good care of yourself," he said. "You are very precious to me and I will be thinking of you all the time you are away."

"I am eternally grateful to you," Zelda replied.

She waved as the carriage drove off.

Then she sat back, feeling she had jumped the first fence in triumph by the very fact that her father and mother had not the slightest idea yet that she was on her way to London.

The Courier the Prince had engaged was an elderly man, who had undertaken the journey very many times. He was recognised not only by the attendants on the train but by the Captain of the ferry.

There was no difficulty in Zelda securing the best cabin and Frau Horwitz was next door to her.

"I have never travelled in such comfort before," she confided to Zelda. "But then they all respect and admire your wonderful cousin."

"He is wonderful to me," Zelda sighed, "just as he is wonderful to his people. I am not surprised they call him *Johann the Good*."

She thought she would call him not only 'good' but every other term of respect and affection she could think of if, when she reached London, she achieved her mission.

It was, however, a long and tiring journey.

*

When they finally reached the railway terminus in London, Zelda, as she had arranged with Prince Johann, managed to persuade her old Governess that she no longer had any need of her services and she went off reasonably happy to stay with her friends.

Eventually Zelda reached Lady Craven's house in Belgrave Square, feeling apprehensive in case things had gone wrong and she was not welcomed as her cousin had arranged.

She need not have worried.

Lady Craven greeted her in a pretty drawing room when she arrived and held out her hands in delight when the butler announced her.

"You have come, dear child, and exactly on time. I was so frightened that something might delay you."

Zelda crossed the room.

Her hostess was, just as she expected, an extremely attractive lady and, although Cousin Johann had said she was nearly seventy, she looked much younger.

She had the kindest and most charming face Zelda had ever seen.

"When I heard from Johann that you were coming to London," Lady Craven enthused, "I was thrilled. Not only to hear from him, but to be able to do something for him. He has always been one of the most wonderful men in the whole world to me."

"That is what I think too," Zelda said. "It is angelic of you to have me, Lady Craven, and Cousin Johann was so certain that I would not be a nuisance to you."

"Of course not, my dear. I assure you I am one of the many people who would be prepared to walk barefoot to the top of Mount Everest if dear Johann asked it!"

Zelda laughed.

"I would as well. Thank you, thank you for having me."

It was rather later after she had dined alone with Lady Craven that she realised her hostess was curious.

She was wondering why she had come to London alone and why Prince Johann had approved her visit.

"When I received his telegraphed message, it was so unexpected," Lady Craven said. "I could hardly believe that you were real and were actually coming to me."

"It must have seemed very rude to have given you such short notice, but perhaps you have guessed that I was running away."

"It did indeed pass through my mind," Lady Craven smiled. "But I could not believe, seeing what a beautiful country you live in, that you should want to leave it."

"I have a special reason for coming to England," Zelda admitted. "But I don't want to talk about it at the moment."

"That is very wise and sensible of you, my dear. You will find, if you tell secrets or gossip about yourself, it flies through the air as swiftly as swallows and everyone knows more about it than you know yourself!"

Zelda laughed.

"What I am really saying is that, of course, I am curious as to why such a young girl should be travelling alone. According to Johann, you are not staying with any relations or with your father's or mother's friends."

"I am running away from them all! And when I achieve all I have come here for, then I promise I will tell you the reason why Cousin Johann has sent me to you."

"I am very flattered that he should have done so," Lady Craven answered. "You must forgive me if I appear inquisitive, but it is the first time he has ever sent me such a charming and delightful visitor as yourself. Or, may I say, anyone so young?"

It was with difficulty that Zelda did not confide in Lady Craven there and then.

She wanted to, but she remembered what the Prince had said.

By the time she went to bed, she had not been in any way indiscreet.

*

Zelda waited anxiously the next day, hoping almost against hope that Prince Johann's letter to Queen Victoria would be answered.

He said he had written to the Queen saying who she was and that her visit was of tremendous importance to her and it would be such a great privilege if Her Majesty would grant Princess Zelda a moment of her time.

He had not actually shown Zelda the letter, but she gathered that he had pleaded with the Queen to invite her to Windsor Castle.

Zelda somehow felt sure, because Prince Johann was of such standing in Europe, that the Queen would not refuse him.

She was actually just starting breakfast with Lady Craven when the butler brought in a letter on a salver and handed it to her Ladyship.

"A message from Windsor Castle, my Lady."

Zelda's eyes lit up.

Lady Craven, as she picked up the letter, smiled.

"I have a feeling even before I open this," she said, "that this is Prince Johann's doing. I have not been invited to The Castle myself for quite some time, so I expect this invitation is for you – "

Zelda did not answer and then Lady Craven opened the letter.

Putting up her *pince-nez*, she read out,

"*Her Majesty the Queen will grant you an interview at three-thirty this afternoon.*"

Zelda gave a cry of delight.

"Cousin Johann has done it!" she cried. "I thought he would, but I was afraid I was not important enough."

"Now we must decide what you will wear," Lady Craven said practically, "and you are a very lucky girl."

"I know that and I am most grateful."

Zelda so wanted yesterday and again this morning to confide in Lady Craven the real reason for her visit.

But her cousin's warning and her own good sense told her that it was all too soon.

It would indeed be a big mistake for her to proclaim that she so wanted to meet the Duke of Milverden.

So she had, with some difficulty, prevented herself from asking Lady Craven outright if she knew him and where he was to be found.

She had reckoned in her own mind that, as he was about twenty-seven or twenty-eight, he might by this time be married or else enjoying the Social whirl of the Season.

Her mother had told her thousands of times what a great success she had been as a *debutante* when she first appeared in London.

And how the invitations had poured in after the first ball she had attended.

"They thought I was a beauty," her mother told her. "And, as the Ambassador's wife was chaperoning me since my mother could not leave my father who was in ill health, I was invited to almost every ball that took place."

"Of course you were presented at Court, Mama."

She knew the Ambassadors always had preference at what was known as *The Drawing Rooms*, at which all the *debutantes* of the year were presented to the Queen.

It was something she had often thought she would love herself, but there had never been any chance of her father wanting to go to London.

So she had to be content with what balls and other Social functions there were in their part of Switzerland .

Yet now she was to go to Windsor Castle and she was quite certain that she was especially privileged owing to the fine reputation of Prince Johann II.

"The Queen disapproves of the way many members of foreign Royal Families behave in what she considers a degrading manner," someone had once said to Zelda.

She thought now that her invitation to visit Windsor Castle was a credit to her Cousin Johann.

The household in Belgrave Square were as excited as she was when they knew where she was going.

The maids all helped in seeing that her clothes were pressed and had been unsoiled by the journey and Lady Craven lent her a necklace of pearls that was bigger than those belonging to her mother.

"Now you look really smart and, I am sure, if they could see you, your father and mother would be very proud of you," Lady Craven sighed.

It flashed through Zelda's mind that her father at any rate would be extremely annoyed that she was seeing the Queen of England without his being told about it.

He had in fact often quoted the Queen when he was presenting Zelda with yet another prospective bridegroom.

"Her Majesty the Queen is becoming known as the *Matchmaker of Europe*," he said. "While she has not yet patronised us, it does seem as though she is tying up all the Principalities with members of her own family."

"I heard someone say that what she is really doing," Zelda added, "is stopping the Russians from taking over the Balkan Principalities and adding them to their Empire."

"I have heard it too," her father had replied. "But personally I don't believe it, as the Russians have certainly left us alone."

Zelda had not answered and she was well aware her father was not interested in any country except his own.

He seldom read the foreign news in newspapers and in fact her father was totally content with life as it was.

He had no wish ever to alter anything, except, of course, he wanted his daughter to bring a Royal Prince or King into his family that would enhance their own image in Switzerland.

When Zelda was finally dressed in a most attractive gown that Lady Craven had chosen from her wardrobe, she put on a small but becoming hat trimmed with flowers.

The whole household came to the front door to see her off.

"You must remember everything Her Majesty says to you," Lady Craven advised, "and do be careful, my dear, not to annoy her. She is very particular about what is said and can, I am told, be very difficult if one does not agree with everything she desires."

"I promise I shall be on my very best behaviour."

She had been half afraid that Lady Craven might be invited too, in which case it would be difficult to speak openly in front of the Queen.

One of Her Majesty's Ladies-in-Waiting had come in a Royal carriage and she had the Queen's instructions to escort Zelda to Windsor Castle.

When they had driven out of sight of the house and Belgrave Square, Zelda turned to her companion,

"It was very kind of you to come and look after me. I hope I will not make any mistakes, but do you credit."

The Lady-in-Waiting, who was quite old, laughed.

"You can be sure of that. In fact I was delighted to come, as I know Prince Johann and actually stayed at the Schloss Vaduz several years ago."

"Oh, how exciting!" Zelda exclaimed.

"You must tell me how he is," the Lady-in-Waiting went on, "and I will give you plenty of messages to take back with you when you return."

"I am sure Cousin Johann will be pleased."

The Lady-in-Waiting was most interested to hear about what was happening in Switzerland.

Zelda told her that in 1864 they had started skiing in St. Moritz and now all the young men were having a try at it and finding the sport very challenging.

"It is something you have attempted yourself?" the Lady-in-Waiting asked her.

Zelda shook her head.

"No, Papa is against it. He thinks it is dangerous and perhaps will attract more people than we really need into Switzerland. Equally he cannot help realising it would bring money into the country."

The Lady-in-Waiting laughed.

"That is what all men always want and seek. So your father eventually will find it is a valuable attraction and indeed I should like to try it myself."

"Then you really must come and stay with us in the winter," Zelda said. "I have a feeling, however, that Papa will still disapprove of women skiing and we will not be allowed to move about except in our snow boots!"

They talked about skiing and other sports until they reached Windsor Castle.

When they did so, Zelda for the first time felt afraid in case she said or did something wrong. If she did, she would surely let down Prince Johann who had been so kind to her.

They arrived in plenty of time and the equerry who met Zelda at the door told her that as the Queen's luncheon guests had already left, Her Majesty would be able to see her very shortly.

There was in fact only a quarter-of-an-hour to wait, before the equerry came to the reception room where Zelda was waiting to say,

"Her Majesty is ready to see Your Highness."

They walked on and on for a very long way down endless corridors before they finally reached what Zelda guessed were the Queens private apartments.

The first door opened for her was a massive portal of oak, picked out in gold and panelled in what she knew was the Gothic style.

The next door was then opened and she went into the Queen's sitting room where the sun was streaming in through the windows.

Zelda's first impression was that the ceiling was extremely high and there appeared to be a great number of photographs on each piece of furniture.

As she walked further into the sitting room, she was astonished, not just by the myriad of photographs but by the confusion of books and *bibliothéque* of every kind.

Then it was impossible to notice anything but the small elderly woman in black sitting by the window.

There was someone else with her.

At a second glance, Zelda realised that it was the Prime Minister – Mr. Benjamin Disraeli.

She had never seen him before, but his pictures had been in every newspaper and she knew that she would have recognised him wherever he had appeared.

As she was presented to the Queen and sank down in a low curtsy, the Prime Minister rose to his feet.

He would have left the room if the Queen had not said,

"Please stay, Mr. Disraeli. I know you want to hear as I do what is happening in Switzerland and the Princess, as you will probably know, is a cousin of Prince Johann of Liechtenstein"

As the Queen finished speaking to him, she turned to Zelda,

"Sit down, my dear, and tell me about Switzerland. It is a country we hear very little about at the moment. I will be interested in everything you have to tell me.

This was something Zelda had not expected.

She first told the Queen how many new and modern ideas Prince Johann had introduced and the Queen seemed especially interested in the manner in which Prince Johann had severed Liechtenstein's economic ties to Austria and had then entered into a Customs Union with Switzerland.

Her Majesty was well informed and every single question she asked Zelda was extremely intelligent.

She felt thankful that she could answer them clearly and sensibly as she had always been keenly interested in everything Cousin Johann was doing.

She also mentioned his extensive art collection and how he was making new acquisitions all the time.

Then the Queen commented,

"That is delightful and it is what I am endeavouring to do myself in England."

While she was talking away, Zelda was aware that Mr. Disraeli was listening intently.

Then, as the conversation appeared to come to an end, the Queen said,

"You must tell me, Princess Zelda, why you have come here so unexpectedly and without your parents."

Zelda drew in her breath.

Instead of prevaricating and evading the question she told the truth.

"To be honest, Your Majesty," she said, "I have come to England because I am anxious to meet the Duke of Milverden."

If she had dropped a bomb in the middle of the room, the Queen could not have looked more astonished.

"The Duke of Milverden!" she exclaimed, "but how can he of all people be of interest to you?"

There was an uncomfortable silence.

Then, as she had started by telling the truth, Zelda felt compelled to continue to do so.

"I have always heard," she said, "that in some way I am personally related to his family."

The Queen looked across at the Prime Minister and there was undoubtedly a smile on Mr. Disraeli's lips.

The Queen then asked her,

"Why should you think that you are connected to the Duke?"

She spoke rather severely.

Yet Zelda thought, having taken one step in the right direction, it was hopeless to try to change the subject.

"To be truthful, Your Majesty," she replied, "there is gossip in Switzerland that I have heard ever since I can remember, that I am in fact the daughter of the fourth Duke of Milverden. Now I am older, I am keen to verify it."

She felt that the Queen drew in her breath and once again she was looking towards Mr. Disraeli.

Then unexpectedly Her Majesty said,

"What you have just asked me, Princess Zelda, is a matter that deeply affects me and also the Prime Minister. So I am going to ask you to be very kind and wait in the anteroom while I discuss the matter with him. Then maybe we will be able to give you an answer to your question."

Zelda was astonished.

Whatever she had expected, it had not been this.

As she rose to her feet, the Prime Minister indicated that she should follow him as he walked across the room.

After curtsying to Her Majesty, Zelda did so.

In the anteroom there was the Lady-in-Waiting and the equerry who had escorted her.

The Prime Minister went in first.

"Her Majesty has asked Princess Zelda to wait here for a few minutes," he declared, "as we have something to discuss. Please look after her until I return."

Then before Zelda could say anything, he had gone, closing the door firmly behind him.

She realised that both the Lady-in-Waiting and the equerry were curious to know what had happened.

But Zelda walked to the window to look out into the garden and then enquired, as if nothing untoward was happening, what were Her Majesty's favourite flowers.

Then she wondered frantically if she had made a terrible mistake and if she would ever learn the answer to her question.

It seemed impossible that Queen Victoria should be aware of the scandal.

She had not thought that it had been talked about outside Switzerland, but there was no denying that the Queen had been astonished at her interest in the Duke, as in a somewhat different way had the Prime Minister.

'What has happened?' Zelda asked herself as she looked out into the sunshine.

She wondered if she had made an unforgivable and foolish *faux pas* or was she, perhaps for the first time on the right track to learning the truth?

CHAPTER THREE

There was a long wait and Zelda began to think that the Queen had forgotten about her and was discussing far more important Affairs of State.

Then at last the door opened and an equerry said,

"Her Majesty is ready to see Your Highness again."

Zelda jumped up.

If it had not been for the equerry, she would have run into the room next door. As it was, she walked with dignity and found the Queen in the same chair as before.

Zelda dropped another low curtsy.

"Please do sit down, Princess Zelda," Her Majesty suggested, "and I am sorry to have kept you waiting."

"I am prepared to wait much longer, Your Majesty, to solve the problem that has been worrying me so."

The Queen looked across the room at the Prime Minister, who then chimed in,

"I think, Your Highness, there is no need for us to prevaricate over the fact that what you are really asking Her Majesty is if it is at all possible that the fourth Duke of Milverden, before he succeeded to the Dukedom, was your natural father."

Because his statement was put so bluntly, Zelda drew in her breath and clasped her hands together and after a moment's pause, she replied,

"That is exactly what I would wish to know, Prime Minister."

"Well, as it happens," the Prime Minister replied, "Her Majesty's late lamented husband, Prince Albert, was a friend of your family and relations and stayed at your house in Switzerland."

Zelda was listening to him wide-eyed.

She was holding her breath and finding it hard to breathe in the excitement of the moment.

"When you were born," the Prime Minister went on, "there was, as you doubtless have heard, a great deal of surprise and talk about it simply because of your father's accident very soon after his marriage."

"That is what I have always heard, but I want to discover the truth."

"My dear late husband, Prince Albert, told me the truth," the Queen came in. "He was in fact particularly interested because the Earl of Milver, as he was then, was a friend of his. He was very anxious that the scandal that arose from your birth should not affect his friend."

"I can well understand him feeling like that," Zelda murmured.

"When he was fatally injured in a riding accident," the Queen continued, "my husband was most upset."

There was a pause before the Prime Minister said,

"I think, ma'am, that Prince Albert was determined that there should be no slur on his friend's name. He therefore pooh-poohed the scandal when it was whispered to him and stated firmly in public that he did not believe for a moment that the child born to the Prince of Brienz was not his own."

"If he said it once, he said it a hundred times," the Queen added, "but naturally like all scandal, especially that which originates abroad, the story was never forgotten."

"And especially when Prince Albert was no longer there to defend his friend as he had always done and as he always did to all his friends."

"That is true," the Queen agreed. "He was a very kind and wonderful person."

There was a sob in her voice and she lifted her lace-edged handkerchief to her eyes.

As if he thought it might be a mistake to linger on this subject, the Prime Minister said quickly,

"Her Majesty and I believe that you have come to England not only to verify your birth, but also to meet the present Duke."

"I would very much like to meet some relations of the man I believe is my real father," Zelda replied. "That is why Prince Johann thought that I should try first to see Her Majesty and receive her advice as to how to do so."

"Very sensible," the Prime Minister said, "and what we have always expected from Prince Johann."

"Indeed," the Queen added, "but things are not as easy, Princess Zelda, as you might imagine."

Zelda looked at her in surprise, wondering what she could mean.

"Because of my dear beloved husband's attachment to the Duke of Milverden who died," the Queen went on, "I was very anxious to be as kind and helpful as I could to the present Duke who succeeded him and who is in point of fact a distant cousin of mine."

"Your Majesty had not met him before he came into the Dukedom?" Zelda asked.

The Queen shook her head.

"No, he was, I was told, always travelling abroad. When the fourth Duke was killed, he came back after the funeral to take his place as Head of the Family."

There was a pause.

Zelda wanted to ask what was wrong, but knew it would be a mistake to try to hurry the story along.

As if he realised that the Queen was still upset, the Prime Minister continued,

"The new Duke is very handsome like so many others of his family. He was an instant Social success as soon as he inherited the Dukedom."

Again there was a pause and Zelda with difficulty prevented herself from asking questions.

After glancing at the Queen, the Prime Minister carried on,

"The new Duke was a little over twenty when he inherited. He was naturally pursued by every ambitious mother and by a great number of beautiful women as well."

Zelda saw the Queen stiffen as if she felt this was somewhat indiscreet and, as the Prime Minister saw it too, he resumed,

"Needless to say, Princess Zelda, his family, seeing that there has been no direct heir to the last Duke, were exceedingly anxious for him to marry."

"I can understand that," Zelda murmured.

She thought as she spoke that the young Duke must have married and they were telling her, in a roundabout way, that the marriage was not a success.

But it would be a mistake for her to say anything as the Prime Minister went on,

"When the Duke turned twenty-two, disaster struck him."

Zelda could not prevent herself from exclaiming,

"What happened? Surely it could not be possible that he too was killed or injured."

"Oh, no, nothing like that," the Prime Minister hastened to reply, "but after listening to the cries of his family and, I am sure of a number of others, all telling him it was his business to marry to produce an heir, he became engaged to a very attractive young lady whose father came from one of the most respected families in the country."

Now the Prime Minister glanced at the Queen as if he thought she would speak, but, as she said nothing, he continued,

"The marriage was arranged and the wedding was to be the most glittering of the London Season. It was to be attended most graciously by Her Majesty herself and other members of the Royal Family."

Again he paused and again with difficulty Zelda prevented herself from asking what had happened.

Very slowly, as if he himself was feeling the drama all too acutely, Mr. Disraeli declared,

"The marriage was to take place in London so that it would be convenient for the Queen and other Royalty, rather than asking them to go to the country. It was when the bride was called on the morning of the wedding that they found she had disappeared."

"Disappeared!" Zelda cried. "But how could she? What had occurred?"

"She had run away with the groom who had always taken her riding and was a trusted servant whose father was in charge of all the family's horses!"

"So what happened then?" Zelda enquired.

"As you can imagine there was consternation. A hurried message was sent to the Queen not to attend the ceremony. But it was impossible to notify everyone and a large number of people turned up at St. George's Church in Hanover Square where the marriage was to take place."

Zelda could understand what a catastrophe it must have been and how appalling for the bridegroom.

"What did the Duke do?"

"As soon as he realised what had transpired, he left England. He stayed abroad for nearly three years, while his family cried copious tears at the disaster. They were, as you can imagine, extremely angry with the runaway bride."

"But I suppose there was nothing they could do."

"Nothing at all, but Her Majesty, when His Grace did return from his journeyings, wanted to welcome him home and make him appreciate that all that had occurred three years earlier was best forgotten."

Zelda looked towards the Queen.

"That was kind of Your Majesty," she said.

"It is what my dear husband would have done," the Queen replied. "But by then he had passed away and was no longer with us."

Again there was a sob in her voice and the Prime Minister went on,

"The scandal over the elopement had of course died down, although people still gossiped about it if ever the Duke's name was mentioned. I suppose in a way it was wise for him to retire to the country and then refuse every invitation he received from Her Majesty and anyone else."

Zelda gave a gasp.

"Do you mean he is a recluse and goes nowhere?"

"I believe he travels when it suits him to different parts of the world, but always under an assumed name. We are told he has no visitors to his house in the country. He does not even answer any of the invitations he receives from those who knew him in London or who were at Eton with him when he was a boy."

"How extraordinary, as it happened so long ago."

"Six years," the Prime Minister remarked.

"Then surely," Zelda persisted, "he should be over it by now."

"That is exactly what we all think, even though Her Majesty has written him a letter begging him to come and see her, he refused, just as I understand he has refused everyone else."

"It is really the most extraordinary story I have ever heard. I am sure that no one at home is aware of it."

Zelda thought as she spoke that even if they did know they would never have told her and it would have prevented the fourth Duke's friends from mentioning him in her presence.

As far as she could remember, all they had ever gossiped about had simply been the fourth Duke's deep affection for her mother.

"So what can you do about him?" Zelda asked.

"That is what we have been discussing," the Prime Minister replied. "Although it seems rather far-fetched and something we should not ask you to undertake, we have a proposition to make. But of course there is no reason why you should accept it."

"*A proposition*?" Zelda repeated.

She looked quickly from the Prime Minister to the Queen and added,

"If it is a question of my meeting the present Duke as I would very much like to do, then naturally I will agree to anything, however difficult it may be. That is why I have come to England."

"Her Majesty can well understand that you are very sincere in your desire to meet the family you believe you are related to," the Prime Minister commented.

He was obviously choosing his words carefully and Zelda appreciated that he was not speaking to her as a Milver, even though the circumstances and the gossip of twenty years suggested that he should.

"It just happens, by one of those odd coincidences, that only two days ago I heard of the Duke in a way I did not anticipate," the Prime Minister added.

Zelda turned to his excitedly.

"What was he doing?" she asked breathlessly.

"He was advertising in *The Times* for a librarian for his house in the country – Minster Abbey it is called. It is one of the most outstanding ancestral houses of England. For years it has been acclaimed for its picture gallery, its magnificent collection of silver and a library I have been told surpasses those of any house in the whole of England."

He paused, but Zelda did not speak.

He was looking at her intently and she guessed what he was about to say.

"You may think this is a strange suggestion, Your Highness, but Her Majesty and I can think of no other way for you to see the Duke or even to approach him."

"You mean – I should apply – for the situation?" Zelda said a little hesitantly.

"Exactly. I imagine you have sampled the amazing library that Prince Johann has at Schloss Vaduz."

"Yes, of course I have, Prime Minister, and I have borrowed his books ever since I could read. When I was with him a few days ago, he showed me the new additions to his library that are absolutely fantastic."

The Prime Minister smiled.

"I thought I was indeed on the right track. What Her Majesty and I suggest, Princess Zelda, is that you write to the Duke, using a false name of course, as a prospective librarian. Or, if you are brave enough to drive up to the front door, you will see him even though he may refuse to engage you."

"Do you think he would do so?" Zelda asked him.

"You are not only a woman, whilst librarians are usually men, but you are also very young and beautiful. I cannot imagine that the Duke will feel that you fit into his monastic life."

Zelda nodded.

"Of course, you are right, I can understand that. But, when I see him and talk to him, it will give me some idea of what my real father may have been like. Perhaps I will then be able to meet some of the other members of the Milver family."

"That will be up to you, but Her Majesty and I can think of no other way that you could even have a glimpse of who you think is one of your relations, unless of course you stand outside his house and hope to see him riding across the fields."

Zelda laughed as he intended her to do.

Then the Queen chipped in,

"I know people who have begged almost on their knees that the Duke should visit them or even asked if they could travel any distance to meet with him. The reply has always been the same. He refuses."

"He not only refuses," the Prime Minister added, "but he does not even reply himself. It's just a brief refusal from his secretary who makes it clear it would be useless to write to him again."

Zelda thought for a moment, then she remarked,

"It just seems extraordinary, Your Majesty, that he should have been so upset, unless he was very deeply in love with the girl he was to marry and who, I imagine, he has never forgotten."

"That may be the reason," the Queen replied. "At the same time I think it was his pride and sensibility that suffered the most. No man likes to be thrown aside for another and certainly not in such cruel circumstances."

"I do see – it must have been very humiliating."

"Appallingly so. He is right in thinking that the Social world will never forget it."

"I am sorry," the Prime Minister now said, "that we cannot offer you any other solution to your problem. I can assure you in the past years that Her Majesty has tried a number of times to be in touch with the new Duke, but he is determined to give up Society and live alone with no one to talk to except for his servants."

"Surely there is someone to keep him company?"

"Her Majesty has made enquiries of a great number of people, especially those who live within easy reach of Minster Abbey. The reply is always the same. His Grace will see no one and only those on his estate have any contact with him."

"Then I can only hope I will be lucky and I thank Your Majesty very much for thinking of anything quite so enterprising. Of course I will call on him and perhaps – who knows – he might even engage me as his librarian."

"I certainly would not bet on it," the Prime Minister said. "Equally you will in fact, if he sees you, be the first person who has seen him socially since he received the news that his bride had run away with another man."

"I feel very very sorry for him, but it is absurd to let his whole life be ruined by one rather stupid girl."

"It does sound strange when you put it like that," the Queen agreed. "As he was so charming and so good-looking it seems a stupid waste that he should shut himself away from everyone who would enjoy his company."

She paused before she continued,

"And of course that he keeps people from seeing the famous Abbey with its superb collection of pictures and so many other treasures that I myself long to see again."

"Your Majesty has seen them in the past?" Zelda asked.

"I was fortunate enough to visit The Abbey when I was very young and I was overcome with the wonder of it. I would love to go again, but there has been no chance of it for so long that I have almost forgotten all that I saw and admired."

"No one has a better memory than Your Majesty of what is beautiful and exceptional," the Prime Minister said tactfully.

"That is what I like to think," the Queen replied with a smile. "But you will realise as well as I do that we should enjoy being able to go to Minster Abbey again."

"So we can only pray, ma'am, that Her Highness Princess Zelda, can open the door for us."

Zelda laughed.

"Now you are asking too much, but if I squeeze in myself and have a peep at all the treasures inside, I will come and tell you all about them when I return to London."

"Then, if you are determined on what I feel is really a wild goose chase," the Prime Minister said, "what I will do is to send to you at Lady Craven's house the cutting from *The Times* in which I read that the Duke was looking for a librarian. After that I leave it all in your hands."

"It is very kind of you and I want to thank Your Majesty more than I can say for your understanding."

Zelda smiled before she added,

"My cousin Johann was certain you would help me however difficult it might be. I know he will be thrilled to know that he was right."

"You must not count your chickens before they are hatched," the Prime Minister warned. "So don't tell Prince Johann anything until you have been to Minster Abbey and either got in through what I might say is the back door or at least spoken directly to the proprietor."

He spoke a little hesitatingly.

"You are thinking that I might be interviewed by someone else?" Zelda enquired.

"I really have no idea, but I don't want you to feel too hopeful. If the Duke has indeed shut out the whole Social world and even Her Majesty the Queen, I think it is unlikely that you will be able to creep in, however small and insignificant you try to make yourself!"

The way he spoke made it sound so amusing that Zelda laughed and so did the Queen.

"Whatever happens," Zelda said, "it will at least be an adventure and thank you, thank you for all your help."

She turned to the Queen as she finished speaking.

"Your Majesty has been even kinder than I could have expected. Wherever else I may go, I will always be thrilled that I have been to Windsor Castle."

The Queen was obviously touched.

"You must promise me one thing," she said. "If you are admitted into The Abbey, I want to hear exactly what it is like inside. Even if you are turned away, do try to see something of its beautiful interior before you leave."

"I will try in every way I can, ma'am. I promise I will see as much as it is possible for anyone to see under the circumstances."

The Queen smiled at her.

"Well, the Prime Minister and I will be waiting anxiously for your report. Perhaps you may, even if it is for only a very short time, become the librarian to the fifth Duke of Milverden."

Her Majesty spoke in a way which made it sound as if she thought it was utterly impossible.

Zelda then curtsied and moved backwards from the Queen towards the door.

She thought as she did so that whatever happened in the future she had at least met the Queen of England and the Prime Minister of Great Britain.

Outside the room the Prime Minister, who had come out with her, whispered,

"I should tell no one, and I mean no one, what you have decided to do."

"Of course not. Cousin Johann was very firm that I must keep myself to myself and not encourage those who are curious as to why I have come to England."

"Prince Johann is certainly a clever and wise man and I hope one day that I shall see him again."

"You must go to Liechtenstein, Prime Minister. He would be so pleased to see you. His Palace is, I assure you, very comfortable, if not as spectacular as this castle."

The Prime Minister laughed.

"Take care of yourself. I think Your Highness is exceedingly brave and I cannot help feeling that in some way you will achieve all that you have set out to do."

"I only hope you are right, Prime Minister."

Then he opened the door into the adjacent room where the equerry and the Lady-in-Waiting still were.

"Her Highness wishes to go back to London," the Prime Minister said. "But I think she would perhaps enjoy some refreshment before she leaves."

"Thank you, but I should return to Lady Craven as soon as I can."

She thanked the Prime Minister again profusely.

Then the equerry took her downstairs to where the Royal carriage was waiting for her.

She shook his hand and stepped into it, as the Lady-in-Waiting joined her.

As they drove off, Zelda waved to the equerry and he waved back.

"You have certainly made a conquest," the Lady-in-Waiting commented, as they drove out of the gates.

"A conquest?" Zelda enquired.

"The equerry said you are one of the most beautiful young women he had ever seen and I know he would have liked you to have stayed longer at Windsor Castle. As you can well imagine, I am curious as to why Your Highness was so long with Her Majesty and the Prime Minister."

"We were just talking about Switzerland."

It was certainly the truth if not the whole truth, but she guessed that the Lady-in-Waiting was not satisfied and she had no intention of confiding in her or anyone else.

If she was to meet the Duke in such a strange and unusual way, she had to be very astute.

On no account must she let anyone know what she was about to do, as it was just possible that the Duke might get to hear of it.

'I will have to think of what I can say and how I can interest him,' Zelda mused. '*And* how I should look.'

When they returned to Belgrave Square, the Lady-in-Waiting, obviously disappointed at not having satisfied her curiosity then refused Zelda's offer of refreshment and insisted on being driven back to Windsor Castle.

Zelda was well aware that she was annoyed. She had failed to extract from her even the slightest piece of information she could convey to others at Windsor Castle. They would undoubtedly be as intrigued as she was.

Zelda now had to cope with Lady Craven.

She wanted to know everything that had happened from the moment Zelda had left Belgrave Square until the moment she returned.

"What did Her Majesty say to you?" Lady Craven asked. "And why was the Prime Minister there too?"

Zelda did not reply and Lady Craven tried again,

"I cannot believe that you were talking only about the political situation in Switzerland."

"I would have been prepared to do so," she replied. "But Her Majesty was not interested in politics, nor did she want to discuss the Swiss Constitution. She was, however, very complementary about Cousin Johann."

"As indeed she should be. At least you will have something to tell him when you go home. I am sure, if she said kind things about him, he will be very gratified."

"I am sure he will," Zelda agreed.

She made an excuse as soon as she could to go up to her bedroom.

She wanted to plan it all out for herself exactly how she could get the Duke at least to see her and that of course would prove the most difficult step of all.

She thought it over very carefully, just as she was sure that Cousin Johann would have expected her to do.

For one thing she was a woman and it was very doubtful if she would even get as far as being interviewed, let alone by the Duke himself.

If he was hating the world and every woman in it, she was far too pretty and he would then feel antagonistic towards her from the very first moment they met.

The one point she had in her favour was that she was very knowledgeable where books were concerned, but would she have a chance to convince him of this?

It seemed to her unlikely.

So she would have to work out a special plan that would force him to meet her face to face.

Although he might well dismiss her on sight with a wave of his hand, she would at least have seen him.

'I have to be clever, I have to be intelligent about this,' she told herself.

But for the moment it seemed impossible and it was like beating with her hands on a bare wall.

When she went down to dinner, it was to find to her relief that Lady Craven had invited a number of friends to meet her.

There were two young men present who made it clear that they found her extremely attractive.

When the ladies left the dining room for the men to enjoy their port, they congratulated Zelda on her gown and her jewels.

"How long is Your Highness going to be staying in London?" one of the ladies asked. "I would love to give a party for you, a big dinner party with a number of people coming in afterwards."

"How kind," Zelda murmured.

And the lady continued,

"Lady Craven will tell you that I have a beautiful ballroom and a conservatory beside it which has listened to many more proposals of marriage than any other place in the whole of London!"

The other women laughed at this.

"You cannot be sure of that, Lucy," one of them said. "But it makes a good story and I certainly know two women who accepted proposals in your conservatory."

"And I know at least a dozen more who have done so," the owner snapped.

They laughed and teased her.

But Zelda was unable to give a date when the party could take place.

"I have one or two things to do outside London," she said, "and I am not quite certain when I will be back. But it is so kind of you to think of it and I would really enjoy such a party, especially if it is given for me."

"Well, let me know as soon as you can when you will be free," the proposer replied.

Zelda promised to do so.

When the guests departed, Lady Craven asked Zelda,

"They told me that you said you were leaving me. When is that likely to happen?"

"In a day or so," Zelda replied. "But I am hoping I can come back to you. There are some people I have to see and I am waiting for instructions as to where they are."

"You make me think they must be friends of the Prime Minister," Lady Craven persisted, "as he is the only person you have spoken to today besides the Queen."

"He does happen to know the person I am trying to find," Zelda replied truthfully.

"Perhaps I can help, my dear, I know most people and for those I don't know, I know the right people to ask."

"You are so kind," Zelda said. "But you have done so much for me already I don't want to worry you."

"But I like being worried – "

Zelda realised that she was curious and it was with difficulty that she managed to get up to bed without saying anything more that would give Lady Craven not only a clue as to whom she was seeking but why she was doing it.

It was a relief when early in the morning when she was first called, she received the letter she was expecting from Number 10 Downing Street.

When she opened the envelope, it merely enclosed the cutting from the newspaper.

Very wisely, Zelda thought, the Prime Minister had not enclosed a letter from himself and she knew, without being told, that he was afraid that she would leave it about.

The advertisement was quite brief,

"*Wanted – an experienced librarian. The applicant must be proficient in European languages. Apply to the secretary, Minster Abbey, Westbridge, Hertfordshire.*"

Zelda read it through twice.

Then slowly, as if she was being drawn to it by a power greater than herself, she saw a plan.

It was set out in front of her mind – a plan telling her exactly what she should do and where she should start.

She was not confident it would be successful.

She could only pray that, although it was now more than one chance in a million, she would gain what she was seeking.

*

The next day she had the difficult task of finding out how she could go to Minster Abbey without of course Lady Craven being aware of where she was going.

This meant that she could not drive anywhere in her Ladyship's carriage.

Suddenly, just like an inspiration, she remembered the Courier who had brought her to London, the man who had been so well recommended by Prince Johann.

He had given her his address, so that she could be in communication with him when she was ready to return. He lived not far away from Belgrave Square.

She told the lady's maid who had accompanied her out shopping and the driver of the carriage that she wanted to speak to the Courier who had brought her to England to arrange a date for the return trip.

She deliberately did not ask him to come to the house in Belgrave Square, as Lady Craven would perhaps stay in the room while she talked to him.

It was far easier to say on their way home from shopping that she wished to call at Number 23 Elmfield Road.

The driver of the carriage knew the way and when they arrived, she saw it was in fact an office where people could make arrangements for travelling.

The Courier who had brought her to London was only one of several and to her relief the man she wanted was available and he took her to a side room where they were alone.

"I want your help," Zelda began.

"You know, Your Highness, that I am here to help you," he replied. "I do hope you are enjoying your stay in London."

"I am. And I don't want to return home just yet."

She thought from the smile on the old man's face that was what he wanted to hear and he was relishing being in London as much as she was.

"What I want to do," she said, "is to visit someone in the country, who is not expecting me, but who I wish to surprise. It would be a great mistake for him to know that I am arriving. Therefore I must trust you completely to keep it a secret until we reach our destination."

"Is Your Highness suggesting that I go with you?" the Courier asked.

"Yes, I want you to do so. But I don't want you to tell anyone where we are going and certainly not discuss with anyone that I am with you."

She thought the old man looked a little bewildered and then he enquired,

"Will Your Highness please tell me exactly what you require?"

"I would require a carriage drawn, if at all possible, by four horses so that we can be there in quick time and be back to London almost before people know we have left."

"Where are we going, Your Highness?"

Zelda had naturally expected this question and she had worked out on a map exactly where Minster Abbey was located.

There was a village near it called Highstone and she thought that if they made for that it would be quite easy at the last moment to turn in at the gates of Minster Abbey.

"What I want you to do," she said, "is to call for me with the carriage at Belgrave Square sharp at nine o'clock tomorrow morning. We will set off immediately for the place I wish to visit and I reckon we will reach it in under two hours."

"Of course this can be arranged, Your Highness," the Courier said. "At the same time I would not like to think I was taking you into any trouble."

Zelda smiled at him.

"I am not doing that and I promise you that Prince Johann would not disapprove of the way I am keeping this particular visit secret."

The Courier gave a sigh of relief and she knew he was frightened of doing anything of which Prince Johann would disapprove.

"I don't expect to be long and I will tell you exactly where I am going when we reach the village of Highstone. In the meantime as far as you are concerned that is our destination and no one should be particularly interested in the journey we are making."

"No, of course not, Your Highness. It just seems a little strange to me that you are travelling without anyone to accompany you."

"That is why I am taking you. I don't trust anyone I am with not to talk. Prince Johann knew before I left that it is imperative my visit to this particular person, who he knows, is kept a secret."

She saw the relief on the Courier's face.

"Bring with you some sandwiches," she suggested, "as we will have no time to stop for luncheon."

She handed him some pound notes having changed some money with Lady Craven.

Then she thought that he might change some of her Swiss money, so therefore gave him the equivalent of ten pounds.

If that was not enough to pay for the carriage and the horses, she would give him more on their return.

"Leave it all to me, Your Highness," the Courier assured her. "I promise you there will be no difficulties and no trouble where my part in this journey is concerned."

"I only hope I can say the same of mine," Zelda said. "Thank you for being so kind and so helpful and do not worry about me. I promise I will not do anything that Prince Johann might disapprove of."

This seemed to comfort the Courier and he kept out of sight as she left the small office and Zelda then climbed into the carriage that was waiting for her.

They drove off and, although she was sure that the lady's maid wanted to be talkative, Zelda was quiet.

She was thinking about tomorrow.

Not only what she should say if and when she met the Duke, but also what she should wear.

On top of which she was wondering how she could impress the Duke, if she did meet him, with her knowledge of literature.

It was lucky, she thought, that she had always had access to Prince Johann's library and her father's was very poor in comparison.

It had been a delight beyond words to be able to pick whichever book she desired from the endless shelves that covered not one room but three in the Schloss Vaduz.

Now, as she thought it over, she was sure that the Duke's impulse would be to dismiss her at once as she was a woman.

She therefore had to impress him with lightening speed that she knew far more than any man he was likely to find in England.

She could remember Prince Johann saying a long time ago that the English people were not great readers and, although they had produced a few fine authors over the years, they could not compare with Greece or France.

'If only he will listen to me,' she reflected, 'then perhaps I can convince him that he is not likely to find a better educated or a more efficient librarian than myself.'

It was something she said over and over again as if she was propelling it on the air towards the man she was determined to impress.

Then, as she gazed at herself in the mirror while she was changing for dinner, she laughed.

No one was going to believe for a moment that a young girl with blue forget-me-not eyes and the fair hair of the morning sun was as erudite as a middle-aged man with doubtless a number of impressive letters after his name.

Someone who would have a large number of people ready with glowing references of his brilliance as regards literature and all that appertained to it.

Then she told herself she would not be defeated.

If that was what the Duke wanted, that was what he would receive.

When she went up the stairs after dinner, instead of getting into bed when the lady's-maid had left her, she sat down at the writing table.

She started to write out her references that she was sure would impress the Duke into at least seeing her before sending her away.

CHAPTER FOUR

With a deep sigh of relief, Zelda put the last sheet of paper she had been writing to one side.

She had written out references that she knew would impress anyone and she thought it over carefully and had deliberately not stated her sex in any of them.

She wrote first of all one from Prince Johann.

In it she said that Giana König had worked as his librarian for five years and had been the best librarian he had ever employed.

As Zelda knew her cousin's signature so well, she signed that reference with Prince Johan's name.

Then she did four more, choosing countries that she thought would impress the Duke.

One of them was Germany where she knew there was a very aged Baron who owned an outstanding library.

She did not forge his signature, but merely said he recommended König as the finest and most experienced librarian he had ever employed.

She wrote more or less the same thing, changing the wording slightly, in Italian, French and Greek.

She invented names for the owners of the libraries other than Prince Johann's. They were all situated in large countries and the Duke could not be expected to be well acquainted with everyone who had an important library.

Putting what she had been writing on one side, she then thought seriously of what she should wear.

Almost as if she was inspired, a conversation she had had with Lady Craven came back to her.

She had been talking about the old days when they were children.

"I do hope," Lady Craven said, "that Prince Johann still has those wonderful Christmas parties that I enjoyed so much. There were also marvellous Nativity plays given by King Frederick William III of Prussia when he was at Neuchâtel."

"I heard my mother talking about those parties and when I was very small we used to have similar parties at home and I enjoyed them very much."

"Of course you did, my dear, and I have them here for my children and grandchildren. Not on the grand scale of Liechtenstein and Switzerland. But we all enjoy them."

Lady Craven paused, as if she was looking back into the past, before she went on,

"I remember once when Prince Johann was quite young and he came to stay with my father and mother, he dressed up as a clown and made us all laugh."

"I wish I could have seen him dressed like that," Zelda giggled.

"As a matter of fact," Lady Craven replied, "his clown's suit is still upstairs in the attic together with all the other costumes we dressed up in year after year. I suppose when I die my children will find some use for them."

She sighed and added,

"But they don't seem to have the same marvellous Christmas parties that I enjoyed when I was a child."

This conversation now came back to Zelda and she looked at the clock.

It was nearly midnight and everyone in the house would be asleep.

The servants, as they were old, slept at the back of the building not upstairs in the attics.

Picking up the oil lamp from the writing table, she carried it to the attic door and opened it very quietly.

As she expected, there was not a sound to be heard in the house and, unlike in many other large houses, there was no night-footman in the hall.

Zelda then walked up the stairs very quietly, her oil lamp illuminating the way.

When she reached the top, there were a number of doors in a long passage and she peeped into two of them to see that they were just empty bedrooms.

Then she came to a third that she saw at first glance was filled with trunks and odd pieces of furniture and there was a large wardrobe at the back of the room.

When she opened it, she saw that it was filled with the clothes Lady Craven had been describing.

There were several garments that could be worn by clowns and one undoubtedly had been for a Fairy Queen.

There were drawers at the bottom of the wardrobe and, when she opened the first one, Zelda almost gave a cry of delight.

She had found what she was seeking.

It was a fulsome grey wig of real hair that she knew she could use as an excellent disguise for herself.

She put the lamp on a table to leave her hands free and in a very short time she had unearthed another wig that was a little darker than the first, also the make-up that had been used by the actors.

What was more important, she found in a cupboard she had not noticed at first, clothes once used by Lady Craven herself.

They were all black and Zelda realised at once that she had worn them when she was in mourning and had then put them up in the attic until she needed them again.

She was only slightly slimmer than Lady Craven and about the same height.

She chose a black coat and skirt that she thought would be suitable for the older woman she was planning to be. They were well made and must have come from an expensive dressmaker.

There were two day dresses, also in black, but with white collars and cuffs and she placed these on the table beside the oil lamp and looked round.

There was a door from this room into the next and, when she peeped in, she saw that there were more props that had been used in the plays.

An old and very lifelike owl with spread wings and some haloes that must have been worn by angels. They would have undoubtedly been for small children attending the Virgin Mary.

There was another large wardrobe in the room and instinctively Zelda went over to it and when she opened the door, she knew she had found what she was looking for.

There were two evening gowns also in black and a black travelling cape and several different hats.

They were just what she wanted, but had wondered how she could buy them. It made it very much easier that she could borrow them.

It was not difficult to find a travelling case to put the dresses in.

However, she realised if she was to take the lamp with her it would mean two journeys.

She hurried down with the case, being very careful not to drop or upset the oil lamp that she was obliged to carry in her other hand.

She put the case down in her bedroom and emptied it and then returned for the hats and wigs and when she had brought them all, she thought how clever she had been.

It was exactly like the answer to a prayer to have everything provided for her when she most needed help.

In her bedroom she then repacked the clothes from upstairs and she found a hat-box in the dressing room where the maids had put her own cases.

She laid the suit out on a chair together with the hat she thought would go best with it.

Then she went to the mirror and tried on the wigs.

She had been correct in having second thoughts in favour of the one that was not as white as the first. It was made of finer hair and she thought that it must have been made for a man.

But when she tucked her own hair underneath it, it was large enough to conceal her fair hair completely and fitted closely onto her forehead.

She was astute enough, however, to realise that she should tie a ribbon round it in the evening, as it would prevent anyone from suspecting she was wearing a wig.

One item she had picked up at the last moment with a feeling of triumph was lying beside the make-up box.

It was a pair of large spectacles that had doubtless been worn as a joke.

She remembered one performance they had given in Switzerland. A very cross schoolmaster was finding it more and more impossible to control the crowd of boys and girls playing round him and his efforts to do so had caused a great deal of laughter.

He had worn spectacles, although she remembered he had been a handsome young man with particularly attractive eyes.

She was sure that when she put these spectacles on they would alter her appearance completely and would certainly hide her eyes that so many of her admirers had claimed were the colour of forget-me-knots.

'How can I have been so lucky to find everything I wanted right here at Lady Craven's?' Zelda asked herself.

She recalled that she had arranged with the Courier to leave early in the morning before Lady Craven was called. As she was a bad sleeper and frequently took a sleeping pill, she did not let her maid come near until she rang the bell and this was sometimes as late as ten o'clock.

Zelda thought that she would be quite safe if she left an hour earlier so that Lady Craven would not see her go.

She therefore rose at seven o'clock and dressed herself in Lady Craven's black suit.

She fortunately had a white blouse of her own that was very pretty, but it was unnoticeable under the severe almost masculine cut of the coat.

Before she finished dressing, she packed some of her own clothes in case she would need them and of course these included her night attire and underclothes.

*

When the maid finally came in to wake her at a quarter-to-nine as Zelda had instructed her to do, she had everything ready.

She was wearing her own cape over the black suit.

"Oh, you're already dressed, Your Highness!" the maid exclaimed as she came into the room.

"I forgot to inform you last night," Zelda replied apologetically, "that I am leaving early. I would be very grateful if you would now run downstairs and bring my breakfast for me."

"Of course, Your Highness."

As soon as she maid had gone, Zelda put one of her own hats on and slipped into a bag the wig, the make-up and the spectacles.

These, she reckoned, because they were so essential to her disguise, she must carry herself.

When the maid came back with a tray, there was only five minutes left for Zelda to eat her breakfast before going downstairs to wait for the Courier.

She had written a charming note to her hostess, saying that she had been invited to a surprise party in the country.

She expected to be away only two or three nights and she knew that Lady Craven would understand that she did not wish to miss leaving London with the young people she would be staying with.

She had therefore had no time to say goodbye, but she would be back very soon and she had left some of her clothes behind, which she hoped would not be a nuisance until she returned.

She thanked Lady Craven again and again and then she put the letter in an envelope to be taken up to her when she awoke.

The Courier arrived exactly as the hands of the clock pointed to the hour and Zelda hurried out to him so that the servants would not have much time to notice him or be aware that he was alone.

The carriage was drawn by four horses as she had asked and her luggage was piled onto the back of it.

They drove away almost before the old butler could realise that Zelda was leaving.

As they moved out of Belgrave Square towards Hyde Park, Zelda exclaimed,

"That was splendid! I had no wish to answer a lot of questions as to where I was going. Now no one has the slightest idea where I will be staying."

"If you are not invited to stay, what happens then?" the Courier asked.

He was obviously still bewildered.

"Then I will come back with you, but I will be very disappointed if I don't see the person I am going all this way to see."

She knew that the Courier was longing to ask her a lot of questions, but was too polite to do so.

They drove out of London almost in silence and the horses were making good progress as she had anticipated.

Finally at ten o'clock she opened the handbag she was carrying and said,

"I am now going to surprise you and you are going to have to be even more discreet and tactful than you have been already."

The Courier looked at her in surprise.

He did not, however, say anything until she pulled the wig out of the bag.

Then his eyes widened and he made an exclamation as Zelda explained,

"What I have not told you and so I am telling you now is that we are going to visit the Duke of Milverden at Minster Abbey."

"The Duke of Milverden!" the Courier gasped, "but I always understood that His Grace never sees anyone."

"That is what I have been told too, but I am anxious to meet him and so I am answering his advertisement for a librarian."

The Courier stared at her.

"But surely, Your Highness, His Grace'll require a man to fill that post."

Zelda laughed.

"You are quite right. Thus, as I cannot pretend to be a man, I am now pretending to be a middle-aged and knowledgeable woman."

He did not answer and she carried on,

"I am going to ask you to sit opposite me and hold this hand-mirror at right angles so that I can put on this wig and make myself look at least fifty years of age."

"I don't believe it possible," the Courier murmured. "Your Highness may be playing a very good joke, but I expect His Grace'll be very annoyed."

"We will have to wait and see, but I am determined to see His Grace for reasons of my own and this is the only way I think it is possible."

She knew as she spoke that the Courier thought it would be completely impossible.

He moved opposite her with his back to the horses holding the mirror in his hands.

Zelda took off her hat and her cape and, having pinned her own hair tightly to her head, she pulled on the wig. On top of it she put on one of the rather plain hats that Lady Craven must have worn at a funeral.

She could see in the mirror that it had altered her appearance to a certain extent.

Yet her face still looked very young and lovely, even though her hair above it was grey, so now she took a crayon out the make-up box and carefully drew little lines beneath her eyes and at the corners of her mouth.

This certainly changed her appearance a great deal and, when she added the spectacles, the Courier began to laugh.

"Your Highness should definitely be on the stage," he chuckled. "I've never seen anyone age so quickly. I swear you'd deceive anyone, even the Duke!"

"What I have to do first," Zelda said, "is to get His Grace to read the references I have as a librarian. If he asks to see me, as I do hope he will, he will be expecting a man."

As she was speaking, she drew out the envelope containing the five references she had written and handed it to the Courier.

"You will ask for these to be taken into the Duke and the servant will obviously assume that they are yours," Zelda said. "He will, I expect, ask you to sit in a waiting room. You will do so until the servant comes back to say that His Grace will see you. It is then you will fetch me and I will go into the room and meet him."

The Courier, who had quite a sharp brain, smiled.

"Only Your Highness could think of anything quite so clever. What you are making sure is that His Grace will not know you're a woman until he's confronted by you."

"Exactly. Then I will have to persuade him to let me stay on as his librarian for at least two or three days. However short or long it is, you must be there to take me back to London when I have to leave."

She thought for a moment and then she added,

"Alternatively, if he is really satisfied with me, then I must stay a week or two and you will be able to go back to London and only return when I send for you."

She knew as she spoke that the Courier thought that she would not be able to keep up the disguise for so long, but he was too tactful to say so.

"We must leave it in the hands of Fate," Zelda said. "But, as we are nearing the village I asked you to drive to, will you tell the driver to take us on to Minster Abbey. I am quite certain that anyone will direct us."

"I expect as he's been driving for a long time," the Courier replied, "he knows the way himself."

He knocked on the glass at the back of the driving seat and the carriage came to a standstill.

Then he leant out of the window and instructed the footman who had climbed down where they wished to go.

He appeared surprised, but he did not say anything. He merely climbed back up and the horses set off again.

"Now let's cross our fingers," Zelda breathed, "and pray that I get what I want, which is to meet the Duke. It is up to you to convince the servant who opens the door that you have important papers for him."

She had put all the references she had written into separate envelopes and then into a big one to hold them all and it was addressed in her excellent handwriting to *His Grace the Duke of Milverden.*

Next they drove through impressive gates tipped with gold and magnificent sculptures on either side.

Zelda was praying anxiously that she would win the battle, but she knew it was going to be a difficult one.

They moved up a magnificent drive of ancient oak trees and, as she saw her first glimpse of Minster Abbey, Zelda realised that what she had heard of it had not been exaggerated.

The Abbey itself had been built in the reign of the early Tudors. It had been closed at the Dissolution of the Monasteries, reopened in the reign of Queen Elizabeth and did not become a private residence until after the reign of Charles II.

It was then presented to the Earl of Milver, who had fought for the Royalist cause with great valour and he had immediately doubled its size and started a collection of pictures and furniture that was to make it one of the most outstanding houses in the whole country.

The Abbey was very beautiful with the sun shining on its windows and all the trees and flowers in the garden made a perfect background.

Zelda could not believe it was real.

It must be part of her dreams.

Then, as they crossed the bridge over the lake and entered the courtyard in front of the house, she felt that the Courier was almost as nervous as she was.

The horses came to a standstill on the gravel.

Almost at the same time the front door opened and they saw an old butler standing at the top of the steps with four footmen wearing the elaborate Milver livery.

Zelda sat back on her seat so that no one looking at the carriage would realise that she was there.

The Courier rose and moved towards the door and the footman who had jumped down from the box opened it.

He stepped out telling the footman to close the door behind him.

He walked slowly and with dignity up the steps to hand the butler the large envelope addressed to the Duke.

As Zelda had expected, the Courier was asked in and presumably taken to a waiting room.

She squeezed herself into the corner of the back seat just in case a curious footman should peep in to see if anyone was there.

Next she closed her eyes and prayed that she would succeed and that after all this striving and planning she would meet the Duke of Milverden.

And then she would be assured, as she almost was already, that she did resemble him and he was indeed her relative.

It seemed to her as if a century passed before there was any reply to the references the Courier had carried into the house.

*

As it happened the Duke was in his library when the butler brought him the envelope and handed it to him on a gold salver.

"What is this?" he asked sharply.

"A carriage has just arrived, Your Grace, and in it a middle-aged man who asked me to give Your Grace this as it's an answer to Your Grace's advertisement."

"Oh, that. What does he look like, Harber?"

"About forty-five to fifty, Your Grace. Quiet and well-spoken."

"Thank you, Harber. I can always rely on you to notice what people who come here are really like."

The butler, who was white-haired and had been at The Abbey since he was a young boy, smiled.

"The one who came yesterday, Your Grace, were a real crook. I be sure of it as soon as I sees the cart he were travelling in. If you ask me, he were spying out the land and we'd have been burgled almost afore he'd left!"

The Duke did not comment and the butler moved to the door to await instructions.

He then opened up the envelope and saw the letters inside.

The first he read was from Prince Johann, as Zelda had intended. He found it very interesting and then read it through again before he turned to the others.

By the time he had reached the Greek reference, he was considerably impressed. In fact he was hopeful that he had found the librarian he really wanted.

"Show this man in, Harber," he called out. "His name is König and he sounds distinctly hopeful."

"That's good news, Your Grace. I'll bring him in."

He left the Duke in the library and without hurrying walked along the corridor.

It was quite a long way to the room where he had left the Courier and, as he expected, the visitor was sitting on one of the chairs reading a newspaper.

"His Grace the Duke'll see you, sir," Harber said.

The Courier rose to his feet.

"That's excellent news," he replied. "I will now fetch from the carriage, the person whose references you have just taken to His Grace."

Harber's eyes opened in surprise.

Before he could say anything the Courier had sailed past him.

He hurried down the steps and opened the carriage door before the footman on the box could jump down.

"His Grace will see you," he said breathlessly.

"You are wonderful," Zelda cried.

She stepped down and walked up the steps to where Harber was standing.

He looked in astonishment at what was happening before his very eyes.

Then, as Zelda reached him, he intoned,

"Be it you, madam, who's applying for the position of librarian?"

He spoke incredulously as if it was just impossible.

"Yes, I am," Zelda responded, "and I am delighted to hear that His Grace will see me."

She spoke to him with a dignity and authority that prevented Harber from arguing with her.

In fact, when she entered the hall, he had to hurry to be ahead of her as she walked towards the far end.

Then, as they went down the passage, she knew he was thinking that the Duke would be extremely annoyed that he had been deceived into having a woman brought into his presence.

When Harber reached the library, he opened the door, but he found it impossible to know how he should announce this unexpected visitor.

So he said nothing.

The Duke, who was standing with his back to the mantelpiece, saw Zelda enter.

He was so surprised that she was not the man he was expecting that for the moment he too was silent.

Zelda walked towards him.

Then she began, speaking clearly, but making her voice a little deeper than it usually was,

"I thank Your Grace for seeing me and I hope you have read the references I have brought you from some of the great libraries I have had the privilege of serving."

"I am very impressed with them indeed," the Duke replied. "But you must be aware that I was anticipating you would be a man."

For a moment Zelda did not speak as if she was surprised.

Then she declared,

"But of course I thought you would have known that Gian, which means John in German, when it had an 'a' added, is a female name."

"I am afraid my German is not as good as it should be," the Duke admitted. "And I never anticipated for a moment that a woman would answer my advertisement."

"I expect," Zelda replied, "they would not have the knowledge I have or had the opportunity to work in such distinguished libraries which have thrilled me ever since I was a child."

"Are you really, even though you are no longer a child, madam, as capable as these references say you are?"

Zelda made a gesture with her hands.

"I can only tell you that I can speak fluently the languages of the countries in which I have served, also the languages of other countries that unfortunately do not have libraries that are as precious as those I have worked in."

"I am certainly impressed," the Duke said. "At the same time it does seem extraordinary that you should be so erudite and a woman."

"I think that is rather unkind, Your Grace. I can only inform you that I read Voltaire in the original French when I was barely out of the cradle."

She paused for a moment before she went on,

"Goethe was read to me instead of the Fairy stories most children listen to and a collection of Dante's works was my parents' present to me on my eighth birthday."

The Duke looked as if he could not believe what he was hearing.

"You cannot expect me to believe that!"

"But it's true and then I was taught Virgil's Aeneid instead of the nursery rhymes that most children enjoy."

The Duke laughed.

"I find all this hard to believe, but equally I will be honest and say I am finding it extremely difficult to find a librarian to cope with my extensive library."

"It does not surprise me, Your Grace. Your library is exceptional in many ways and I have always heard that your Folios of Shakespeare are unique even for England."

"They certainly are," the Duke agreed. "And I am very lucky to have so many of them."

"You are indeed, Your Grace. I will be honest and say that even Prince Johann, whose library is famous in Europe, could not equal all that I have heard about yours."

"That is just what I want to hear," the Duke said. "I would like you to look round for a moment and see the library for yourself."

He walked away from the mantelpiece as he spoke.

Zelda turned round not to look at the library but at the Duke himself.

He was exceedingly tall and handsome.

She knew instinctively, not only from what she saw of him, but from what she felt vibrating from him, that he was in fact her relative.

Her journey had not been in vain.

"What I want to show you and what I am really rather doubtful about," the Duke was saying, "is this book of Homer which has troubled my ancestors as to whether or not it is genuine."

"Please let me see it, Your Grace."

The Duke took a book from one of the shelves and put it into her hands.

It contained the Iliad and the Odyssey of Homer in Ancient Greek and the book itself looked old and battered.

Zelda took it in both of her hands.

As she had done often before when she was alone in a library, she closed her eyes and tried to make her own vibrations touch those that came from the book.

She did not speak, but she realised that the Duke would be looking at her with surprise.

After a few moments had passed, she said,

"This book is old, very old, but if it purports to be one of the very first printed editions of Homer, published in 1488, it is definitely not as old as that."

The Duke smiled and took the book from her.

It had been the test he had used many times before and he had found there were few men brave enough to tell him that the first book he handed them was actually a fake.

He showed Zelda more books in his collection.

She did not gush over them or make a particularly complimentary remark about any of them, but he knew that she was thrilled at seeing so many outstanding works.

She seemed to have, he thought, a strange affinity with them that he could not explain even to himself.

They moved about the library for nearly two hours.

Then the Duke suggested,

"I understand you arrived in a carriage and I expect the coachman will want to know whether you will stay or return to wherever you have come from."

"I am hoping I may stay," Zelda replied, "simply because your library fascinates me. You know as well as I do that it would take days to look at it all and appreciate everything that has been collected over the centuries."

"Do you really think that you could handle such a vast library?" the Duke asked her.

"I have handled those that are nearly as large and, as you know, satisfactorily," Zelda answered. "I would love to see for the first time in England that the English can equal the French and Italians, who always give themselves such airs when it comes to literature."

The Duke chuckled.

"I know that is true. The Germans particularly are determined that they will have, if they try hard enough, a better collection than this one."

"I very much doubt they can, Your Grace. But we must certainly prevent them from doing so, otherwise they will become cock-a-hoop and will feel they have taken you down a peg or two!"

The Duke was astonished that she should speak to him in such a way.

At the same time he could not help laughing.

"I would suppose," he said, "you have your own ideas about how we should go looking for new additions to this collection."

"Of course I have, Your Grace. As a matter of fact I know there are some small libraries in Italy and France where they have no idea of the value of their possessions, but they would be a welcome addition to any library."

"Then I must certainly go and look at them – "

There was a moment's silence and then he drew himself up to his full height and added,

"Although it is something I never expected, I would be grateful if you would come here on a trial basis. If we do not agree after, shall we say a week or so, then we part without any animosity on either side."

"I accept Your Grace's invitation," Zelda said. "I agree that if we don't get on, then we must surely admit it immediately and I will leave in the same way as I arrived."

"That seems to me satisfactory. Are you prepared to stay now or will you have to go back to wherever you have come from to collect your luggage?"

"I have it with me, Your Grace. I will just speak to the Courier who has brought me here and tell him that if it is necessary I will be in touch with him."

She walked towards the door as she spoke.

The Duke made no attempt to accompany her.

He merely sat down in a chair nearest the fireplace and wondered to himself whether he had made a terrible mistake in allowing this unknown female into his house, whether or not she was indeed as exceptional a librarian as she sounded.

He had no idea that Zelda had with some difficulty prevented herself from dancing along the corridors that led to the hall.

'I have won! I have won,' she told herself with a somewhat undignified air of triumph.

Now at last she would be able to solve her own problem.

CHAPTER FIVE

Having sent the Courier away after thanking him profusely, Zelda jubilantly walked back to the Duke.

Then, as she went back into the library, her instinct told her that he was at that moment almost regretting the decision he had made.

She therefore enquired in a very quiet voice,

"Would you like me to start by looking over these books or has Your Grace something particular to show me first."

The Duke reacted exactly as she had hoped.

"I think," he suggested, "you should come round The Abbey and see the other collections I have here and then afterwards you can start work on the books."

"I would love to, Your Grace."

She thought as she spoke she must remember to always speak in a deep voice, otherwise he might think her younger than she appeared.

"I think that we should start first with the picture gallery," the Duke proposed.

This meant their going upstairs to the long gallery, where Zelda knew there were some superb pictures.

While the Duke expected her to be knowledgeable about books, he had not expected that she would know so much about pictures as well.

But Prince Johann's pictures – the finest in Europe – had taught her a great deal.

She then managed to say something interesting and original about every artist whose pictures they examined.

Because the Duke had been alone so much, he was delighted to find someone who could talk on his favourite subjects – and who apparently knew as much if not more than he did.

They spent at least an hour in the long gallery and then they went into two smaller galleries. One contained all the earliest artists in the collection, the other the latest.

"That is clever of you," Zelda exclaimed, "because people don't like to show their ignorance in asking the date of an artist even though they greatly admire his pictures."

The Duke did not reply, but she knew that he was about to say that no one saw his collections except himself.

However, she quickly turned to one of the pictures they had not yet discussed and told him several snippets he did not know himself about the artist.

When they had finished with the pictures, he took her into the main reception rooms which she thought very beautiful, but equally it was obvious that they were not being used.

There were no flowers anywhere for one thing.

In one of the drawing rooms the Duke had to pull back the curtains and open the shutters before they could see the furniture that was early French and very valuable.

"It would be a grave mistake to let the sunshine in on these pieces," he said. "So I have told the servants to leave the curtains drawn."

Zelda made no comment and they moved on to the other rooms, all of which were to her mind fantastic and in most cases were finer than she had ever seen elsewhere.

It was after five before they returned to the library.

Zelda realised that, having had a luncheon of only sandwiches while they were travelling, she was now very thirsty.

She was just about to ask the Duke if it would be possible to have a cup of tea when he volunteered,

"I suppose I was rather inconsiderate in taking you on such a long tour of the house after you had made the journey here from London. Would you care for some tea?"

"I was just thinking that my throat was dry and I am feeling rather thirsty," Zelda replied.

"You must forgive me," he said, "but because you were so interested in all I have shown you and in fact you are the first person I have taken round this house for years, I forgot that you are after all a human being."

"I would hope so, Your Grace, but it is rather late for tea and I don't want to be a nuisance."

"I will tell you what we might have, which I would enjoy myself, is a glass of champagne."

"I will certainly not say no to that offer," Zelda replied.

The Duke then opened a door that led into what was obviously a study where she thought he must spend most of his time. It certainly looked considerably more lived-in than the other rooms they had visited.

In one corner there was a grog table on which was an ice bucket with an unopened bottle of champagne in it.

"I suggest you sit down" the Duke said to Zelda, as he walked towards the table. "Again I had forgotten while we were talking so interestingly that you are a woman and not a man and suggested you had a rest a long time ago."

Zelda guessed he was really thinking that she was old and her legs might be aching, as she sat on the sofa.

But she did not speak while he opened the bottle of champagne and brought her a glass.

She sipped it slowly, thinking it a tonic she really needed after such a long day and at the same time being so nervous in case she failed and had to return home without having seen the Duke.

He sat down on an armchair facing her.

Now she was able to look at him in a way she had been too shy to do as they were moving around the house.

There was no doubt, she reflected, that his square forehead was a replica of hers and, although his eyes were a deeper blue, they were almost identical in shape.

She wondered that if she took off her spectacles whether he would notice it.

He was indeed strikingly handsome and she could understand why he had been such a success when he first appeared in the Social world.

It was ridiculous that he should have buried himself here surrounded by such exquisite beauty.

Yet, however glorious all his pictures and furniture were, they could not talk to him.

The Duke finished his glass of champagne and said,

"Let me give you some more."

Zelda shook her head.

"No thank you, Your Grace. I am no longer thirsty, but I am looking forward to dinner."

As she spoke, it suddenly struck her that, as she was only engaged as a librarian, she would not be dining with the Duke.

And being a step above the servants, she presumed therefore that she would dine alone.

Again, as if he was following her thoughts, the Duke proposed,

"I think, unless you wish to be alone, it would be nice if we dined together tonight and I can tell you more about my plans for the future."

"I should be delighted to accept your invitation, Your Grace, but I would not wish to upset the routine you usually keep."

"Naturally I dine alone and think about what I can do to improve the library. If you will dine with me, we can talk about it and you can then give me your opinion as to whether or not I am on the right track."

"Thank you very much," Zelda replied demurely. "Now, Your Grace, I would like to go to my bedroom. I think I should rest a little before I change for dinner."

"Of course," the Duke murmured. "I should have thought of it myself."

He crossed the room and pulled at the bell-rope that hung from the ceiling.

A few moments later, almost as if he was waiting outside the door, Harber appeared.

"Your Grace rang?"

"I want you to take – "

The Duke hesitated and Zelda realised that she had not told him whether she was a Miss or a Mrs –

"Mrs." she said quickly and the Duke went on,

"Mrs. König to her room. As she has had a long journey, we will dine at seven-thirty."

It was with difficulty that Zelda did not laugh at the surprise on Harber's face.

He had never for a single moment anticipated that someone who was only to his mind a paid servant would dine with the Duke.

With difficulty he managed to blurt out,

"In the large or small dining room, Your Grace?"

The Duke hesitated for a second before responding,

"The large dining room, Harber. We have not used it for a long time. But I want Mrs. König to see it and this will be a good opportunity."

"Very well, Your Grace," Harber replied, still in some confusion.

He waited at the door and Zelda knew that he was ready to escort her to her bedroom.

"I must thank Your Grace," she said, "for the most interesting and delightful tour we have just made. I want to think about it and discuss it with you later."

"I will look forward to it, Mrs. König."

Zelda turned round and walked to the door and, as she stepped into the passage, Harber followed her and they walked towards the staircase.

"I expect, ma'am, you're aware," Harber said as they reached the first step, "that His Grace always changes for dinner."

"I thought he would," Zelda replied, "and I have in fact brought an evening gown with me."

She thought the butler was amazed that it was not a shock to her to be invited to dinner the first night she had arrived.

But he said nothing.

Instead he led the way along the landing to where she guessed the State bedrooms would be situated.

At the end of one of the corridors an elderly woman came out of a room and Zelda was almost sure it opened onto the Master suite.

She was dressed in black with a silver chatelaine at her waist and Zelda knew that she was the housekeeper.

"I am looking for you, Mrs. Saunders," Harber said, "because I thinks you should know that Mrs. König, who is staying here as librarian, has been invited to dine with His Grace tonight."

Mrs. Saunders held out her hand to Zelda.

"I was told you'd arrived," she said in a somewhat superior tone. "But I didn't expect you to be eating with His Grace."

"It is very nice to meet you," Zelda said, shaking her hand. "As I am very experienced as a librarian, His Grace and I have a great many matters to discuss."

The housekeeper and Harber exchanged glances and Zelda could guess what they were thinking.

"I had put you on another landing," Mrs. Saunders said. "But I think now you'd be more comfortable here on the main floor and you'll have a boudoir attached to your bedroom where you can work when you're not engaged in the library itself."

"That is very kind of you and I am sure it will be very helpful."

"Then if you'll come this way, ma'am, I'll show you to the room I've now chosen and Mr. Harber'll be kind enough to inform the housemaids that your luggage is to be brought to the Princess Elizabeth room."

As she was speaking, Mrs. Saunders was walking ahead towards the other end of the corridor.

She had almost reached the top of the stairs when she stopped and opened a door that had a crown in gold above it.

When they entered, it was obvious it had not been used for years and Mrs. Saunders pulled back the curtains and the shutters and then she opened a window that let in a little fresh air that Zelda thought was badly needed.

"This room was used by Queen Elizabeth before she came to the throne," Mrs. Saunders informed her, "and there's another room by the Master suite that Her Majesty used when she stayed here after she were crowned."

"How fascinating!" Zelda exclaimed. "I feel most honoured to be allowed to sleep in her room."

She reckoned as Mrs. Saunders was speaking that the housekeeper was thinking it was a pity that a great number of rooms were not slept in.

She then moved past the huge gold-canopied bed and opened a door in the wall.

"This leads into the boudoir," she said, "where I expects, Mrs König, you'd like to have your breakfast."

It was a most attractive boudoir and Zelda looked round her with delight.

"I have never seen a more beautiful room," she enthused. "I hope when you have the time, Mrs. Saunders, you will show me some of the other State rooms. I have always heard now beautiful they are in English houses and I will be fascinated to compare them to others I have seen overseas."

"What country do you come from?" Mrs. Saunders enquired.

"Actually Switzerland, but I also spend a great deal of time in Liechtenstein."

"Then it'll certainly be a change for you to come to England. I expects it will be very different here to those countries."

"It is in many ways. But of course in the Royal Palace, like that of Prince Johann of Liechtenstein, they have a magnificent library and many of the State reception rooms are nearly as impressive as those I have seen here."

Mrs. Saunders looked as though she felt this could not be true, but she looked gratified.

By the time Zelda had looked round the boudoir, her cases had been placed in her bedroom.

She had locked them, so the housemaids had not yet been able to unpack.

"If you'll give my girls the keys," Mrs. Saunders suggested, "they'll unpack for you."

"That is very kind of you," Zelda replied, "but as I may not be staying long, I would rather unpack myself and just take out the things I will need."

She had been carrying in her hand the bag in which she had put the wig, the make-up box, the hand mirror and the spectacles she was wearing on her nose.

She knew it would be a mistake for the housemaids to investigate her belongings just in case they thought what they found was strange.

She had put in a few of her own clothes as well as the black dresses belonging to Lady Craven and as her own clothes were very pretty, she knew that the housemaids would find the contrast rather curious.

"Oh, well," Mrs. Saunders was saying, "if there's nothing you want, I'm sure you'd like to lie down on your bed for a rest before dinner."

"As dinner is at half-past seven, I will not have very long, but I would be grateful if I could have a bath."

It was only when she had spoken that she realised it was unusual for someone who was not in the upper classes to have a bath and, without looking at the housemaids, she knew that they were both astonished.

"We've not provided a bath for this room for many years," Mrs. Saunders said. "But there's no reason why it shouldn't be done. So now, girls, tell the footmen to bring the hot water upstairs and you fetch the bath from where it stands next to the linen cupboard."

The two housemaids went off to do what they were told and Zelda sensed that they looked at her in surprise before they left the bedroom.

She was acutely aware that now Mrs. Saunders was extremely curious about her and she was sure she intended to ask her some searching questions.

She therefore took off her hat and coat.

"To be honest I am extremely tired, Mrs. Saunders, It has been a long journey from London and His Grace has walked me a long way round this very large house."

"Very well, I'll leave you, Mrs, König. But you only have to ask me if you want anything. If you need one of the maids to do up your dress, ring the bell by the bed."

"Thank you very much, you are very kind."

Zelda waited until Mrs. Saunders had left and then she opened one case and took out all that she required.

She locked it up again, as she had no wish for the maids to see her pretty lace-trimmed nightgown, as it was certainly so different from what they would expect of her.

As they were all thinking of her as a servant, she had to be careful.

Putting on her negligee, she lay down on the bed, placing her spectacles beside her so that she could put them on at a moment's notice and she was most careful not to disarrange her wig.

She was more tired than she realised and although she had a great deal to think about, she was almost asleep when a short while later her bath was brought in.

The two maids set it down in front of the fireplace, which was where it was usually placed in great houses, even in the summer when the fireplaces were filled with flowers and not coal.

Then a footman carried up large cans filled with hot and cold water and put them in the room.

"Do you want us to stay with you, ma'am?" one of the maids enquired when everything was laid out.

"No thank you," Zelda replied. "I am well used to looking after myself and thank you for bringing me my bath. I certainly need it after driving from London."

The maids smiled at her and, when they had left the room, Zelda locked the door.

Then she climbed into the bath and really enjoyed the warmth of it.

Finally when it was nearly half-past seven and she knew that she must not be late, she rearranged her wig and put the black ribbon round it that she thought it might need when she saw it in the attic.

It certainly gave her a more glamorous appearance and she thought, despite the colour of her hair, it made her look quite pretty.

Then she added the lines under her eyes and at the sides of her mouth.

She did it very carefully and put on her spectacles before she rang for a maid to do up the black gown she had chosen to wear.

However, when she put it on, she felt it was much too smart – it had obviously come from one of the most fashionable Bond Street dressmakers.

It was of black chiffon that floated round her and it was not at all aging and the *décolleté* was decorated with tiny diamante she knew would glitter in the candlelight.

It was with difficulty she prevented herself from putting on the diamond necklace that had belonged to her mother.

She had brought it with her not because she had expected to wear it, but simply because she thought it was safer with her than if left in London and she would have been miserable if she had lost it or it was stolen.

Instead she wore a demure double row of pearls with a large one that dropped down in the front and, as she was supposed to be a married woman, she knew that she could wear pearl earrings.

She had been sensible enough to remember to wear her mother's wedding ring when she left London and now she added a single pearl ring to it, feeling that it gave her hands grace in the same way the dress graced her body.

Now she was ready.

She took a last glance at herself in the mirror to be quite certain that she looked the age she pretended to be.

At the same time she could not help thinking that she looked very unlike a professional librarian and she only hoped her appearance would not make the Duke curious.

He was waiting for her in the same room where they had enjoyed the champagne.

He looked, she thought, in his evening clothes even more handsome and certainly more dashing than he had when she arrived.

She knew from the expression on his face that he was surprised at her appearance. He had quite obviously not expected her to be wearing such a smart gown or to be ornamented with pearls round her neck and in her ears.

"Oh, there you are, Mrs. König!" he exclaimed, as the butler had opened the door for her. "I was hoping you had not fallen asleep out of sheer tiredness and forgotten we were dining together."

"I had not forgotten, Your Grace," Zelda replied. "I feel rested and I am now feeling very hungry."

The Duke laughed.

"Well, I hope the cook is aware of that. I eat very frugally when I am at home. In point of fact I have cut several courses off my meals."

"I would have thought it quite unnecessary for you to do so, Your Grace, as I expect you ride to keep your figure. But you must be a disappointment to your cook."

She saw that the Duke had not thought of this and for a moment he looked surprised.

He offered her a glass of champagne before he said,

"I am sure, as the staff know that I have company tonight, there will be enough food to satisfy your appetite however big it may be."

She did not answer and then he asked,

"What is the food in Switzerland like?"

Zelda smiled.

"I would much rather you ask me what I would eat in France. I was in Paris a short while ago and they had some new dishes that were absolutely delicious. I became, while I was there at any rate, exceedingly greedy!"

The Duke chuckled.

"I would agree there is no food to equal the French chefs. But now you have made me nervous as to whether you will not only be disappointed but embarrassingly harsh about our English menus."

"I will certainly tell you the truth after dinner," she replied. "May I say I am drinking the health of the French in this delicious champagne and you know as well as I do, Your Grace, that no country in Europe can equal it."

"That is true," the Duke agreed after a moment's thought. "Equally the Germans try to make a good wine, but I doubt if it will ever rival the French."

"Of course the Scots have their whisky, which is superior to any other spirit obtainable," Zelda remarked.

The Duke looked up in surprise.

"How do you know about the Scots?" he asked. "You cannot tell me you have been a librarian North of the border as well, because I will not believe you!"

"No, I have never been to Scotland, but I have read a great deal about it and I feel that there is so much in that country I should automatically respond to."

She knew as she spoke that there was a great deal of Scottish blood in the Milvers.

In fact, if she was not mistaken, her grandmother was a Scot and so were many of the Duke's predecessors.

"You continue to surprise me, Mrs. König. I was wondering when I was dressing for dinner how you could speak our language so well and not be English and how you have crammed so much into your life especially as you are a married woman. Have you any children?"

It was a question Zelda had not expected him to ask her and she therefore hesitated before she replied,

"No, I have none, which is very sad. I always think children bring a joy and excitement into one's life that one cannot find in any other way."

There was a distinct pause and the Duke remarked,

"I wonder if that is really true."

"Of course it is, Your Grace, every man and woman should realise their life is incomplete unless they produce a child to take their place when they die."

The Duke turned towards the grog table to pour himself another glass of champagne.

She knew she had made him think that, in cutting himself off from his family and refusing to listen to those who urged him to have an heir, he was actually missing something very important.

'Because he has made the decision to live his life alone,' Zelda mused to herself, 'he does not want to talk about it.'

She was wondering what she should say now when to her relief Harber announced that dinner was served.

"I deliberately did not show you the dining room when we were looking round," the Duke said, "because I think it is one of the most attractive rooms in the whole of the house. It is the room where the monks received their visitors and where the Abbot sat in State."

They walked a long way down the main passage. The great doors at the end of it were appropriate for the entrance into a grand dining room.

It was an incredibly large room with long windows looking onto the central courtyard round which the house was built.

There was a magnificent Medieval fireplace and the long refectory table was ornamented with gold candlesticks and gold goblets studded with jewels.

The whole room was lit only with candles, many of them in huge gold candlesticks over five feet high and the room glowed in their light.

Zelda thought it was undoubtedly one of the most exciting rooms she had ever seen.

As the Duke sat down at the end of the long table and Zelda sat on his right, she asked,

"How often do you eat like this, Your Grace, and feel that at the very least you are a King."

The Duke laughed.

"I admit I have not eaten in this room for years. It was clever of Harber to make it ready so quickly in your honour."

"I am not only grateful for the compliment but I am entranced by the room itself. You must tell me all about it. I am sure its history is as enthralling as it looks."

The Duke related how the monks had left at the Dissolution of the Monasteries and how they then returned when Queen Elizabeth came to the throne and The Abbey then became more influential than it had ever been before.

"I suppose the Roundheads must have done a great deal of damage," Zelda asked him.

"It would help me to tell the story if I knew more about the Roundheads," the Duke said. "The historians in England always seem to start their history about the reign of Queen Anne and ignore what happened previously."

"I feel that is rather scathing, Your Grace, but I am really interested in this wonderful building and I only hope you will sit down and write a book about it if there is not one already at hand."

"There are such books available undoubtedly, but I have never thought of writing one myself."

"Why not, Your Grace. I feel that you know more about this house than anyone else and of course you should put it all down on paper."

"It is certainly an idea," the Duke reflected.

"It is not only a necessity," Zelda persisted, "but an obligation as far as you are concerned, Your Grace."

She was speaking as she would have spoken to any one of the Statesmen she had met with Prince Johann.

But the Duke looked at her in surprise.

"Are you telling me what is my duty?" he enquired. "Surely that is unusual on such short acquaintance."

"I had heard quite a lot about you before I arrived," Zelda answered. "But no one had described to me in detail the wonder and beauty of this house."

"Now you are saying exactly what I want to hear, Mrs. König."

They talked on about The Abbey and its history all through dinner, which Zelda found quite delicious. It was certainly far better than anything she would have had in Switzerland.

It seemed sad, she thought, that the cook usually had only one man to cook for and she had therefore done her very best when for the first time in years the Duke was entertaining a visitor.

When dinner was over, they did not return to the room they had occupied before.

Instead they walked into one of the drawing rooms where the chandelier had been lit by Harber and there were candles on the mantelpiece and candelabra on the tables.

Even the Duke looked rather surprised when Harber opened the door and showed them in.

"I never thought of going into the Queen's drawing room tonight," he said. "I am sure, Harber, it will delight our visitor."

"It is absolutely wonderful!" Zelda exclaimed. "I think we are the two most spoilt people in the whole world to have such a beautiful room all to ourselves."

"The coffee is by the sofa, Your Grace," Harber piped up.

Zelda sat down while the Duke poured out a liqueur and put it beside her.

"This has been an exquisitely enchanting evening," Zelda sighed. "Thank you, thank you, Your Grace."

Then turning to Harber, she added,

"Please will you thank the cook for me for the most delicious dinner."

"I enjoyed it too," the Duke said, "and I know cook will want to give us the same another evening."

The butler left the room and the Duke sat down with his liqueur in his hand.

"I have enjoyed showing you my house and talking about it," he said. "I want you to be completely honest and tell me if you can suggest any improvements. I realise how experienced you are not just with ancient books but with everything of value. Therefore, be honest with me and tell me of any mistakes I have made."

There was a pause and then Zelda replied,

"I can only think of one, Your Grace. It is in fact a big mistake and one which I think one day you will regret."

The Duke looked at her in a puzzled fashion.

"What can that be?" he enquired.

"It is this, I think that you are the most selfish man alive, Your Grace," Zelda answered quietly.

He stiffened and looked at her in astonishment.

"What do you mean?" he demanded.

"Exactly what I say, Your Grace, you asked me for the truth and I have given it to you. How can you keep all this beauty, all this marvellous history, all these priceless and unique treasures all to yourself?"

There was silence and then the Duke asked,

"Do you really mean that?"

"Of course I do, Your Grace. If you want me to elaborate, although you may be angry if I do so, I would say also that you are wasting your own life and your own brain. You have so much more than almost anyone else to give the world and yet you bottle it up here behind closed doors."

She paused, but the Duke did not speak and so she went on,

"You have deliberately thrown away all the wonder and excitement in your own life and denied other people the unique glory that can be found everywhere here in Minster Abbey."

Again there was silence.

Then the Duke rose and walked to the window.

Almost roughly he pulled back the red curtains and stared out into the garden.

Zelda did not move or speak.

She could see the moon shining in the sky above, casting a silver light over the ground below and even from where she was sitting she could see how beautiful it was.

Then she asked herself if she had now made a huge mistake and the Duke would tell her to leave tomorrow morning.

He might even throw her out tonight.

Yet she had felt the words come to her mouth so easily and it was almost as if someone was telling her what to say – someone who knew even better than she did what a crime the Duke was committing in barring his doors to the outer world.

Ten minutes must have passed before the Duke turned round.

As he looked at Zelda, he crossed the room and sat down again in the same armchair.

"I suppose," he began, "I should feel insulted by what you have just said to me. But instead, after all we have talked about this afternoon, I want to argue about it. I want to have your opinion and you have to convince me that it is better than mine."

Zelda wanted to laugh, but instead she smiled.

"If I have to go then I must go," she said, "but I had to tell you the truth. You are too big a man to be lied to. So I merely said aloud what was in my mind."

"That is what I want to hear, but, as you are aware, few people would be brave enough to say aloud what they are really thinking."

"I am sure a great number of people despise you for what you are doing and a great number are ready to cry."

"Why should they do that?" he asked.

"Because, if you saw a great artist throwing away his brushes and claiming that he would paint no more or a magnificent pianist closing down the lid of his piano and refusing to open it again, would you not think it a waste of their talent."

"It's easy to talk like that. When I decided I would withdraw from Society where I had been humiliated and insulted, I went round the world. I found a great deal to delight me and make me forget to a certain extent all that I had suffered."

"If the world gave you that privilege, Your Grace, how much have you given in return?" Zelda enquired.

The Duke was silent until he said,

"I suppose that you are implying that I should write a book on The Abbey and its history?"

"You can do that, Your Grace, but you have much more to give."

"You mean that I should allow people to see what is in this house?"

"I mean giving your country, your brain and the person that is *you*. Everyone of us was born of love. We therefore ought to give back a certain amount of the love we have received and which should have increased within us while we were growing up. I don't mean only the love of a man for a woman and a woman for a man, but the love of children and the love of animals."

She paused before she continued,

"It is all part of each one of us and to deny that to the people who need it is a cruelty that none of us should be wicked enough to perpetrate."

She spoke very quietly and she was surprised when the Duke rose from his chair and walked not again to the window but to stand in front of the mantelpiece.

"Why have you come here," he asked, "to say all this to me? Why are you torturing me by telling me quite clearly I am selfish and wicked to withdraw from the world into the peace and quiet of this venerable house – ?"

He spoke angrily.

As his voice died away, Zelda replied softly,

"You should know the answer to that, Your Grace. Perhaps because I have been too hasty and too outspoken, I should leave you now to think, not about my impertinence – for I am of no consequence at all in your life – but about yourself and how very very important you are."

She said the last words very clearly.

Then she walked to the door and went out, closing it quietly behind her.

As she walked slowly upstairs to her bedroom, she asked herself if she had destroyed what might have been a good friendship between herself and the Duke.

Whether or not that would happen, what she did know unmistakably was that her father had indeed been the Duke's relation.

And that the blood of the Milvers ran in her veins.

CHAPTER SIX

In her bedroom Zelda stood for a long while at the window looking out into the garden.

She wondered if she had made a terrible mistake and if she should have kept her thoughts to herself until she was ready to leave.

Now she was almost sure that the Duke would tell her to go in the morning and she would leave The Abbey ignominiously without actually telling him the reason why she was there.

In reaction to the thrill and excitement of seeing the wonderful house and talking so intently to the Duke, she now felt frantically that he would definitely send her away.

That would mean she would never see him again.

If he was so angry that he just sent her a message by the servants, it would be too late then to tell him who she was and why she had come.

'How could I have been so silly?' she asked herself.

Leaving the curtains drawn back so she could see the moonlight, she undressed and put on her nightgown.

Then she thought that perhaps she would write an apology to the Duke. She would say that she was sorry she had been so outspoken and hoped he would forgive her.

'It is the least I can do,' she told herself, 'because I really behaved very stupidly.'

She went into the boudoir and because there was no light, she pulled back the curtains.

She found a piece of beautifully engraved writing paper with the Milverden crest printed on it.

It was difficult to know what to say.

She just wrote how sorry she was that she had upset him and how much she admired all the sublime beauty he had shown her that afternoon.

She wanted to say that she enjoyed talking to him at dinner more than she had ever enjoyed a meal before, but she thought that was being too familiar.

She did not read through what she had written, she merely signed it and thought that she would send it to the Duke the next morning after she was called.

She then remembered that he had said he was riding early in the morning and they would therefore not start work until ten o'clock.

'Perhaps when he is riding he will forget what he thinks is my rudeness,' Zelda mused to herself.

She decided she would let her note reach him when he came back to breakfast.

Then she went back to her bedroom and stood for a while gazing out of her window at the moonlight on the garden.

It was long after midnight, in fact it was getting on for two in the morning when finally Zelda decided that she must try to sleep.

She had told the maid to call her at eight o'clock, but she thought that was now quite unnecessary.

The Duke had said they would start working at ten o'clock, in which case, if she was to have all her wits about her, she must try to sleep.

She returned to the boudoir and scribbled a note for the maid,

"Please bring me my breakfast at nine-fifteen. I do not want to be disturbed until then."

She opened the door and put the note outside and then she locked the door as she had before – it would be a disaster if the maid came in early and saw her without her wig.

Finally she climbed into bed, still feeling upset and desperately worried that the Duke would dismiss her first thing in the morning.

'I would like to have ridden with him just once,' she reflected wistfully.

She knew it would be fascinating to see the estate and she was quite sure it would be prosperous and just as perfect as the house.

In fact there would be nothing for her to find fault with except the Duke himself.

She tossed and turned thinking how much she had enjoyed her dinner with him and she was sure that it was something exceedingly special that would never happen to her again.

'He is the most interesting and exciting person I have ever met,' she thought. 'How could I have been such a fool as to upset him the first night we were together?'

She had not pulled back the curtains to cover the window.

And when finally she fell asleep, the moonlight was fading and the dawn was creeping up over the trees in the distance.

*

The Duke was called as always when he was going riding at seven o'clock.

His valet brought him tea and some pieces of very thin bread and butter.

This had always been a tradition and the Duke had made no changes where his household was concerned.

When he returned from his ride, there would be a large breakfast waiting for him downstairs in the room he always used when he dined alone.

His valet brought the morning newspaper and laid it on the table beside the bed with his tea.

The Duke poured out his tea absentmindedly while he looked at the headlines.

He liked to be aware of what was happening in the outside world he had abandoned and so every newspaper published was delivered every day to The Abbey.

The paper his valet had brought him that morning was *The Morning Post* in which he always read the account of the day's proceedings in the Houses of Parliament as well as news from abroad.

Today's reports seemed to be rather dull.

He turned over the page and to his consternation saw the name 'Minster Abbey.'

He found he was reading a report of a conference concerning William Shakespeare that had taken place that week at Trinity College, Cambridge.

The Duke learnt that there had been a meeting of Shakespeare's admirers at which a number of distinguished academics had spoken.

Those speaking for Trinity College had boasted that their library contained the finest collection in the world of Shakespeare Folios and Quartos with the exception of the collection in the library at Minster Abbey.

The Duke was frowning as he read on.

He knew that the first Folio was a collected edition of Shakespeare's plays issued by a group of booksellers in 1623. In this eighteen plays were published for the first time together with another eighteen plays that had already appeared in editions known as Quartos. Three more Folios of the plays were subsequently published at intervals.

The Trinity College speaker had gone on to say,

"*The Quartos I would like Trinity College to own more than any others are 'Romeo and Juliet', published in 1597, as well as 'A Midsummer Night's Dream', published in 1600.*"

The Duke was becoming increasingly annoyed.

"*Those,*" the speaker rambled on, "*and I believe, although I am not sure, 'Hamlet', which was published in 1603, are now in the library of Minster Abbey, where alas they are never seen. I believe that with them are many more treasured Quartos and I am sure I am right in saying there is also a copy of the Third Folio published in 1664.*"

The Duke read and re-read the report several times and his annoyance was rapidly turning to anger.

He felt that this speaker had no right to refer in that way to his library, especially when there was no chance of it, like everything else he possessed, being examined.

He threw the newspaper down on his bed, stood up and started dressing.

His valet poured out warm water for him to wash in and then helped him into his riding breeches.

He himself tied his stock round his neck and then his valet brought in his riding coat, which was well cut and made him look even more distinguished.

"I'll go down, Your Grace," the valet said, "and see if Your Grace's horse be at the front door."

The Duke did not answer.

He was still fuming at what had been said at Trinity College and how infuriating it all was.

Then, as he picked up *The Morning Post* from his bed, he had an idea.

He walked out of his room and down the passage to the door of the boudoir that was attached to Zelda's room.

He opened the door intending to put it on the table where he knew she would have her breakfast.

But the curtains were drawn back and he thought that perhaps she was already awake.

He wondered if he should tell her that there was a report he particularly wanted her to read in the newspaper.

Then, as he crossed the room to go to the table, he saw the door into her bedroom was half-open and he could see that the curtains in the bedroom were drawn back and the sun was pouring in.

She was obviously awake.

He reached the communicating door and pushed it open a little further before he asked in a low voice,

"Are you there, Mrs. König?"

There was no reply and he thought that perhaps she had already gone downstairs.

He had at the moment no wish to talk to her, feeling it would be rather embarrassing after what had been said last night.

It had in fact passed through his mind he should dismiss her.

Then he knew that she was without exception the most interesting person he had met for years.

Their conversation at dinner had been positively scintillating and he had found himself laughing as he had not laughed for a long time.

He had had to strive to keep his own end up when they were discussing books and places abroad, of which he found she had a surprising knowledge.

Without really thinking what he was doing, he then pushed the door open even further.

He next became aware that, despite the drawn-back curtains over the window, she was in bed and he could see her head quite clearly on the pillow under the gold canopy.

He hesitated, wondering whether he should put the newspaper he was holding in his hand on the bed or leave it on the dressing table.

Suddenly the Duke noticed that the head he could now see under the canopy of the four-poster was the same colour as the sun climbing up the sky outside.

It flashed through his mind that perhaps Mrs. König had left The Abbey and her place in this room had been taken by one of the servants.

But he could never imagine in his wildest dreams anything like that happening at Minster Abbey.

Yet why was this person in bed not Mrs. König?

Instinctively and without even thinking about it, he drew nearer.

Now he saw lying in the bed the most beautiful girl he had ever seen in his whole life.

Her glorious golden hair was falling over her bare shoulders.

Her eyelashes were dark against the pink and white translucence of her skin.

For a moment the Duke thought that he must be dreaming or seeing a vision.

Then he realised that the girl, who seemed so small in such a large bed, was definitely alive and breathing.

He thought he himself must be deranged.

How could this be Mrs. König?

The grey-haired bespectacled woman with whom he had talked and argued until she had told him what she believed to be the truth about himself.

Could this possibly be her daughter, whom she had brought into the house without his being told?

Was it possible he had been so easily deceived into believing the woman he had engaged as his librarian was not actually all she appeared to be?

He stood staring down at the sleeping girl.

Then he thought that in some strange way her face, beautiful as it was, was familiar.

Somewhere, somehow he had seen her before.

Yet this was not possible.

She was deeply asleep and her one hand, which was lying outside on the lace-trimmed sheet was undoubtedly, he surmised, the hand he had noticed the previous night when they were talking over dinner.

Like most women she had used both her hands to express her feelings.

Almost automatically the Duke had thought that her hands with their long thin fingers must belong to someone with blue blood in her veins.

He had thought at the time that when he knew Mrs. König better, he would ask her to tell him more about her family and herself.

How was it possible, unless she had generations of scholars and the very best education behind her, that she could be so knowledgeable?

Yet now, when she was only a young girl, not much older than twenty or twenty-one, it seemed to him almost a miracle that she could know so much.

Not once but a dozen times he had been surprised as they walked round The Abbey.

She had discussed subjects with him that he could not expect anyone so young to know anything about.

He stood there staring down at Zelda.

Again he felt that he had somehow seen her before.

Then she made a little movement in her sleep and he became aware of the position he was now in.

Hastily he walked back to the communicating door and only when he reached it did he turn and look back.

Zelda was still asleep.

But now her hand was thrown out at one side and it was exactly the age-old gesture innumerable painters had striven to depict on canvas.

For a long time the Duke stared at her across the room.

Then he went out silently, putting the newspaper, as he had intended to do, on the table in the boudoir.

He let himself out into the corridor.

As he walked past Zelda's bedroom door, he saw the message she had left for the maid.

This finally persuaded him he was not dreaming or imagining her.

She did indeed actually exist, and what is more she had deliberately disguised herself as a middle-aged Mrs. König to deceive him.

But for what reason?

Could it be that she intended to defraud him of some of his treasures, but it was impossible for him to believe that this was her intent in coming to The Abbey.

Yet the question mark was there so large and so irritating that he knew he would never rest until he knew the truth.

Only when he was riding away from the stables on one of his most outstanding thoroughbreds did he try to think clearly and sensibly of what he should do.

How was it possible, he now asked himself, that he should have been so easily deceived by a woman?

He supposed the real reason was that he had not seen any of them for a long time.

Because he had been so entirely beguiled by Mrs. König's knowledge and experience, he had not thought of her as a woman – rather as someone who appreciated the value and uniqueness of the treasures he owned.

She could speak to him on equal terms on subjects he had never been able to discuss with anyone else for six long years.

'If I confront her,' he thought to himself as he rode across the green fields, 'I will only frighten her away and then perhaps I will never know the truth.'

At the back of his mind he kept feeling that her face was familiar to him.

There was something about it that reminded him of someone he could not put a name to and yet he was almost sure he was using his memory and not his imagination.

He rode on for over two hours and then slowly he turned back.

He had thought of nothing else when he was riding except Giana König, but had come to no conclusion.

The one issue he did accept completely was that he had no intention of sending her away until he had found out the truth.

It would be unbearable to wonder for the rest of his life why she had come to The Abbey and exactly why she had taken so much trouble to deceive him.

He stopped there.

He felt that he had the answer to this question.

Had she arrived looking so young and so beautiful, he would not have thought of engaging her, nor would he have listened to anything she had to say to him.

It was obvious that she had expected him to turn her away because she was a woman and then it was only because she had been clever enough to appear more than twice the age she really was that he had been deceived into engaging her, at least on approval, as his librarian.

'It was a clever move, extremely clever,' he said to himself. 'What I have to find out is her reason for coming here to The Abbey in the first place, unless it was in some subtle way to rob me.'

It was something he had been afraid of ever since he inherited and so he had taken immense care to protect every room until The Abbey was almost a fortress against thieves.

All the doors locked and so did the shutters from inside and he himself inspected all the safe-guards at least once a week.

He had refused the idea of nightwatchmen and his servants were, he thought, far more professional at the task than any imported nightwatchman could be.

As he had told Mrs König, at least three quarters of the house was kept clean but not used and the rooms where the most treasured pieces stood were locked so effectively that it would have taken any burglar hours of hard work to cut his way into any of them.

Yet now, when he had least expected it, there was a stranger at Minster Abbey.

A stranger with a brain equal to his own.

But in fact she was young, beautiful and must be an imposter.

'What am I to do? What the devil am I to do?' the Duke asked himself as he rode home.

At the same time he was intrigued.

It was something unusual for him to think about and puzzle over and it was a problem with no easy answer.

When he eventually reached the stables, the grooms were waiting as they always were to take his horse.

"I hopes you've had a good ride, Your Grace," his Head Groom asked.

"Very good and Silver Sword was superb."

The Head Groom smiled at the praise.

At the same time the Duke knew he was thinking it was a pity there were not more people to admire Silver Sword and to watch him win, as he undoubtedly would, the Grand National.

The Duke had actually had a battle with himself against entering his horses for the National or the Gold Cup at Ascot.

He felt if they won, it would only draw attention to himself.

People would be aware he still existed as far as the Social world was concerned and he just wanted them to forget they had ever known or heard of him.

He thought he had managed that very cleverly by shutting himself away by himself in The Abbey when he was in England and by travelling incognito when he was abroad – not as a Duke but under an assumed name.

He often congratulated himself on being so subtle and he was quite certain that the Social world had forgotten his very existence.

And yet now this woman, who he had thought was elderly but actually was young and beautiful, had dared to challenge him and to tell him he was being what she even called 'wicked'.

'If I had any sense,' the Duke thought as he walked back to the house, 'I would tell her to leave The Abbey and never think of her again.'

But he knew he could do so.

Before he sent her away, he must have an answer to the question of why she had come to see him and why in disguise.

Breakfast was waiting for him in the small dining room he had used for every meal until dinner last night.

Because he had wanted to show Mrs. König how beautiful the large dining room was, on an impulse, he had ordered that they should dine there.

Now, as he helped himself from an assortment of dishes, he was suddenly anxious to see her again.

To make quite sure that he had not been dreaming when he had seen the beautiful girl asleep in the bed.

He drank his coffee.

Then he forced himself to walk more slowly than he wished to do down the long passage to the library.

*

Zelda had come downstairs earlier than ten o'clock for a breath of fresh air in the garden before she went to the library.

The garden was just as entrancing as it had looked from her bedroom window and she thought the sun shining between the trees and turning the water thrown up into the sky from the fountain into a rainbow was a picture she would always remember.

'If I stay here too long, I will never want to go back to Switzerland,' she mused. 'But of course I may be sent away today and will always regret everything I have not yet seen.'

For one point they had made rather hasty visits to the small picture galleries and she was quite certain that there were many more fantastic pictures in the bedrooms and sitting rooms that she had not yet viewed.

'It's all so perfect in its own way,' she thought as she walked back to the house.

The front door was open and there were only two footmen to smile at her as she walked in.

"It's a lovely day," she remarked. "I expect you are wishing you could be by the lake and maybe swimming in it rather than in attendance here."

The two footmen smiled.

"We're gettin' a bit old for swimmin' now," one of them said. "When I were a boy, I used to swim even when it were winter."

"That is what is making you so strong now," Zelda commented.

Then she walked across the hall and down the long passage that led to the library.

It was at that very moment she remembered that *The Morning Post* had been on the table with her breakfast.

She had, however, not read it, but told the maid to bring it to the library for her, as she wanted to read it when she came back from the garden and now it was lying on the writing desk.

*

She was reading the report of the meeting at Trinity College when the Duke walked in.

She saw at a quick glance that in his riding clothes he looked even more handsome and distinguished than he had last night.

At the same time she had only to think of last night for her eyes behind her spectacles to become very wide and questioning.

"Good morning, Mrs. König," the Duke began. "I hope you had a good night."

"Yes, thank you, Your Grace. I was just reading this newspaper. I expect you have read about the meeting that took place yesterday at Trinity College, Cambridge."

"I wanted you to read it," the Duke replied. "That is why I left it in your boudoir."

Zelda looked at him.

Then she was aware that she had left on her writing table the letter she had written to him last night apologising for all she had said to him.

She had actually forgotten about it this morning and had gone straight to breakfast and had not remembered it was waiting on the writing desk.

"I am extremely perturbed by this meeting," the Duke was now saying, "and the reference to the fact that I possess many Shakespeare Quartos."

"You have not yet shown them to me," Zelda said in a quiet voice. "As you can imagine, I am longing to see them."

"As I think a great many other people will now be," the Duke added angrily.

She did not answer and after a moment he asked,

"Are you still thinking about how wicked I am and accusing me of depriving other people from handling my books as well as all my other possessions?"

He spoke sharply, but Zelda laughed.

"Of course I don't expect you to let people handle any of your possessions. Please forgive me for what I said last night, Your Grace. I have written a note apologising to you, but then I forgot to give it to the maid earlier."

"There is no need to apologise, Mrs. König. I am only wondering why, when you have such a low opinion of me, you wish to be my librarian."

Zelda smiled.

"When I applied for the position of librarian here, I expected to attend to the books not to Your Grace."

It was a clever answer and the Duke had to admit she had climbed out of that one very skilfully.

"I find it just extraordinary," he said, walking to the mantelpiece, "that you are so knowledgeable on so many subjects. Are you so rich that you have been able to travel to so many places? How did you first start to realise that books were your prime interest in life?"

He longed to add –

'Rather than men who you should be thinking about at your age.'

There was a pause before Zelda responded,

"As I have already said, I have been lucky enough to enjoy libraries that are almost as good as yours. But at the moment we should be thinking about this Shakespeare meeting and what they have said about your possession of his Quartos. If your books are in danger, then you have to be ready to prevent them from being stolen."

"I think that is most unlikely. I have taken every precaution to make the house burglar-proof. What worries me is the number of people who will either call or write to me, asking if they can examine the Quartos the speaker mentioned, especially as they are the most popular ones like *Romeo and Juliet* and *A Midsummer Night's Dream*."

"I very much agree with you, Your Grace, and they are my favourites too. In fact I am longing more than I can possibly say to see them and hold one in my hands."

She spoke so eagerly that he forgot for a moment everything but his pleasure in his possessions.

"Let me show them to you," he suggested. "You will agree that I am very fortunate in owning the Quartos, which I would certainly choose myself for my most prized possession if they were all paraded in front of me."

He took her to a place in the library where the third Folio and the Quartos were arranged.

He was not surprised when Zelda gave a cry of sheer delight when she also found Shakespeare's Sonnets.

"These were printed in May 1609," the Duke told her. "There are 154 sonnets and a poem entitled *A Lover's Complaint.*"

"It is a poem I have never read," Zelda admitted, "and I am curious to know what his complaint can be."

Because she spoke so excitedly, the Duke could not help asking,

"What would *your* complaint be if you had a lover, or, perhaps I should say, when you have one?"

It was the sort of question Zelda enjoyed and which Prince Johann had often asked her.

"I suppose that the worst complaint one could have about one's lover would be if he loved someone else," she replied.

"I suppose, if you were very beautiful, that could not arise – "

"I think," Zelda said, as if she was working it out for herself, "a man always looks for beauty in the woman he loves, while a woman judges a man more by his mind and his heart."

The Duke looked at her.

"I wonder if that's true?" he exclaimed.

"I think if a person has real love for another, their appearance does not matter too much. Love is something that vibrates between them and a woman should feel that it is the man's heart that is beating for her, rather than his eyes thinking she is more beautiful than the other women he has met before."

She spoke very slowly and then she made a little gesture with her hands.

"I am explaining it rather badly, Your Grace, but I think you know what I am trying to say."

"I am surprised that you should speak hesitatingly about love when you are extremely fluent and balanced in what you say about everything else."

Zelda was about to reply that she was not at all knowledgeable about love because she had never been in love.

Then she remembered that she was supposed to be a married woman.

Once again as if he had a suspicion of what she was thinking, he asked,

"Tell me what you felt when you first fell in love. It was, I suppose, a long time ago. But you must be able to put into words what made you fall in love and if you were aware that the man in question was loving you for your looks rather than your heart."

For a moment Zelda was intrigued by the question and longed to give the Duke an answer that was not only true but provocative.

Then, as if she realised the danger of speaking of love when she was supposed to be old, she said quickly,

"I think, Your Grace, there is so much work to be done here that I should settle down and continue, before talking about Shakespeare and your exciting possession of his Quartos."

The Duke was amused at the way she was twisting herself out of an awkward situation, but at the same time he was now even more intrigued than before.

He showed her his copy of the Third Folio and the Quartos and she agreed with him that they were in a safe place at the far end of the library.

"It would take a bomb to open these windows," the Duke boasted proudly. "Therefore everything I possess of Shakespeare is, I assure you, quite safe."

"I hope you are right, Your Grace. We must sit down and wait for the letters that will pour in begging you to allow mobs of students to come knocking on the door."

"Whatever you may say and whatever you may think, Mrs. König, I have no intention of letting them in. It would be a terrible mistake for Shakespeare or any other of my special possessions here to be handled by strangers or even talked about."

Zelda did not answer and after a moment, he added,

"Can you imagine, whatever you may say about my being selfish, what this place would be like if the public were admitted and tramped round making the place dirty and grubby? And failing to appreciate the beauty of it all."

"I agree that you have a point there," Zelda replied. "But I still think that within reason those who really care and understand about your treasures should be allowed to see them."

"I thought last night you were putting *me* on show rather than my treasures."

"That is another story altogether. As you are not as angry with me today as I thought you might be, I suggest we ignore that problem until we can find a solution to it. It should not be too difficult if we both concentrate our brains on *you*, Your Grace."

The Duke laughed as if he could not help it.

"That is the one thing I want to avoid," he grinned.

"I know that, Your Grace. But you know as well as I do, if you try not to think about an issue it is the one thing you always remember."

"You are certainly the most extraordinary woman I have ever met," the Duke sighed. "In fact, when I look at you, I feel you cannot be real and are merely part of my imagination."

There was a pause before Zelda managed to say,

"Actually I am alive and breathing, and you can be sure of one thing, I will not vanish into oblivion until you tell me to do so!"

"I wonder if I can be certain of that!"

"The answer to that is only time will tell," Zelda said. "Of course you may find me an encumbrance if I stay here for years. But you have to admit there are years and years of work in front of us."

The Duke glanced around the library.

It was all too true that it had never been properly catalogued and the inventories that had been made were out of date and the books had often been re-arranged.

He looked at Zelda and remembered how beautiful she had looked in bed and how young.

"Are you really prepared," he asked, "to catalogue this whole collection in the way it should be done?"

"Shall I say," Zelda replied after a pause, "that I will do my best? But, if I am unable to complete it either to your satisfaction or to mine, then I will admit defeat."

"That's a good answer, Mrs. König. Now having shown you what I have of William Shakespeare, I suggest you tell me whose plays and poems you consider to be the best, thinking of course at the moment of English authors. Then I will say if I agree with you."

He knew as he spoke that the idea delighted Mrs. König. There was a sudden glint behind her spectacles that told him she was intrigued.

Then he had an almost uncontrollable desire to pull off the wig from her head and see her looking as beautiful as she had looked in bed early this morning.

It was with difficulty he controlled himself.

Then, as he walked down the library towards the place where he knew most of the poets had been put in the past, Harber appeared at the door.

"Excuse me, Your grace," he said to the Duke, "but there's a number of gentlemen here who say they'd like to examine the Shakespeare Folio and Quartos as was written about in the newspaper this morning."

The Duke glanced at Zelda.

"Here you are. I believe you have magicked them up just to annoy me!"

He turned to Harber.

"Tell the men, whoever they are," he said, "that my library is not available to anyone and see that they move down the drive and off the place as quickly as possible."

"That's what I expected Your Grace to say," Harber replied, "but they be very insistent."

"Make it quite clear that no visitors are admitted into The Abbey under any circumstances and they are to get off my land immediately."

He snapped the last words at Harber and he moved away rapidly.

"It is just what I might have expected from that damn silly speech in Cambridge," he fumed.

"They might be students," Zelda said, "and you can hardly blame them for wanting to improve their knowledge of William Shakespeare, who after all is one of the greatest authors the world has ever known."

"Well, they are certainly not going to increase their knowledge of him by handling my Folios and Quartos!"

"You cannot blame them for asking, Your Grace. "Nothing ventured, nothing gained. They may not even be English students, but perhaps have come from abroad and are spending their time travelling in search of knowledge."

She paused before she continued,

"Actually I only heard the other day that they have discovered some wonderful sculptures in Greece that had never been noticed and would gradually have crumbled away if it had not been for the diligence and persistence of archaeologists who were searching for such treasures."

The Duke, who had his back to her, turned round.

"So you are on *their* side. You would like to let in all those hooligans and sightseers to spoil the quiet and beauty of my house and undoubtedly would sooner or later damage its contents."

"I very much doubt if they would do so," Zelda said. "Equally, if you do not allow them to see what you have, what will happen eventually? When you die without a direct heir to inherit, you may be succeeded by a relation who does not truly appreciate the value and beauty of your collection."

The Duke was listening and her voice sharpened as she went on,

"It may then be sold off bit by bit or perhaps fall into ruin simply because no one bothers about it."

"So you would really let in these people who are waiting outside?" the Duke asked her furiously.

"I would at least find out who they are and where they all come from and if they are genuine seekers after knowledge, but of course, if you are determined to keep everything for yourself, they will have to wait until you are dead. That is, if they are not dead first."

She spoke almost angrily, because she thought that he was being not only selfish but also rather foolish about his beloved possessions.

He had sworn not to have an heir of his own and how could he be certain what sort of person would take over from him?

The collection had already passed through a great number of hands without being ruined.

A few people had been able to see The Abbey in the past, so just why could they not do so in the future?

As if the Duke sensed what she was thinking, he declared indignantly,

"It is not only what I possess that I don't want to show to the public. I don't want to meet them myself and I have reasons for making that decision. So don't annoy me by trying to change my mind on an entirely personal matter that is no one's business except my own."

Now the Duke was really angry.

Zelda, without another word, walked quietly back the way they had come and out of the library shutting the door behind her.

Only when she had gone did the Duke realise that he wanted her back.

He wanted to go on talking to her.

In fact he had to admit he did not want to lose her.

CHAPTER SEVEN

As she walked slowly upstairs, Zelda wondered if now she had really burned her boats.

Perhaps she would receive an abrupt message in a few minutes ordering her to leave the house!

Because she was afraid that was going to happen, she deliberately went to the picture galleries as she wanted a last look at the Duke's wonderful pictures.

There were so many she longed to see, but had not known where they were.

She paused for several minutes before one of the Michelangelos and again in front of a particularly beautiful Rubens.

Then she glanced out of the window and saw that the Duke was once again riding.

He was going, she thought, over the fields as if he intended to travel some distance.

She went back downstairs.

When she entered the hall, Harber said,

"I were just coming to look for you, ma'am. His Grace had a call from one of the farms where there be a fire and he's gone off at once to see what's happening."

"I am sorry about that," Zelda replied.

She thought, however, it gave her a chance to go back to the library and start work.

It was obvious the Duke had said nothing to Harber about her leaving and so she should therefore be doing the job she was employed to do.

She went straight to where she knew the Quartos were and what she really wanted to do was to sit down and read them.

On second thoughts she decided that they could be in a safer position as far as possible from a window and, despite what the Duke had said, someone might manage to smash a window and quickly find what he was seeking.

She therefore moved them all to the other side of the library where there were no windows and placed them carefully high on a shelf where they could not easily be picked up by anyone who had no right to be there.

If there were visitors, and the Duke was generous enough to receive them, he could easily lift down one copy at a time and then put it back out of reach of anyone who was not very tall.

This took her some time and luncheon was ready before she had finished.

As she ate alone, she thought what fun it had been last night and how she had managed to make the Duke laugh as well as to argue with him in a hundred different ways.

'I have never met anyone quite so interesting,' she thought, 'and, with the exception of Cousin Johann, so knowledgeable.'

Once again she was thinking how stupid she had been to upset him – she should have at least waited three or four days before she criticised anything.

Her only hope was that, as he had not ordered her to leave immediately, she would perhaps be able to stay at least a little longer before she returned to London.

*

The afternoon passed slowly.

Tea came, but there was still no sign of the Duke.

"That there fire must be a lot worse than His Grace feared," Harber commented as he waited on her.

"How was it possible for the farm to be set alight?" Zelda asked.

"They didn't say when they called, only that the fire were raging and one of the stacks of hay was making it worse than it had seemed at first," Harber informed her.

"I only hope all the animals are safe."

She was thinking that on most farms there were not only sheep and lambs but chickens and of course cows as well as horses.

"Now don't you worry yourself," Harber said. "You can be certain His Grace'll get things working right as soon as he arrives. If anyone can save the place from burning to the ground it'll be His Grace."

"I am sure he will be very efficient," Zelda said.

*

When the Duke returned, it was after six o'clock.

He walked into the library just as Zelda was putting away the notes she had made during the day and tidying her desk.

"You are back, Your Grace!" she exclaimed as he walked in. "I wondered what had happened to you."

"I have been working like a dog to put that fire under control," the Duke replied. "At least the farmhouse is saved."

"I am so glad. Harber was right when he said you would soon organise everything."

"Needless to say the fire precautions were out of date and far too scanty. Although I did send for the Fire Brigade, they did not arrive until the worst was over."

"What about the animals?" Zelda asked.

"We saved them all right. It's just a question now of building new barns and of course housing the animals."

He was obviously in good spirits and Zelda thought it was because today he had had something definite and demanding to do.

It was a terrible mistake for a man of his age to get up in the morning and know, after he had gone riding, that there was no pressure on him to exert either his body or his brain.

As she thought that he had now told her all about the fire, she said,

"I hope you will be pleased with my efforts while you have been away, Your Grace."

"What have you done?"

There was a suspicious look in his eyes as if he felt that she had thrown open the door to a crowd of strangers.

"What I have done," Zelda said quickly in case he should be angry, "is to move your Shakespeare treasures to another place. I thought after all that had been said in the newspaper this morning that they were too near a window which might be smashed open if people were determined to rob you."

"That was very intelligent of you, Mrs. König. I did not think of it myself. But where have you put them?"

"On the other side of the room, high up on a shelf."

The Duke nodded as if he was pleased and then he walked across the room to the grog table.

"I have really earned a drink today," he said, "as I missed both luncheon and tea."

"I think you will find that Harber has brought in some *pâté* sandwiches," Zelda said. "He is wonderful the way he thinks of everything."

"He thinks about me and has spoilt me ever since, as a little boy, I was sometimes brought here on a visit and used to go into the pantry to beg for a sweetmeat."

Zelda laughed.

"You have certainly rewarded him now as he runs the whole house and I am certain that everyone obeys him because he speaks for you."

"He was only a boot boy in those days, but he rose quickly to footman, then first footman and ended up as you see overlording the house and even me when I let him!"

"I don't think he aspires as high as that."

"You would be surprised how servants, when they have known you for a very long time invariably bully you into taking more care of yourself than you want to!"

Zelda thought of her old Governess, who had most certainly ruled her with a rod of iron.

Then she commented,

"You are quite right and I am always grateful for what they have done for me, even though at times I have kicked over the traces."

The Duke chuckled.

"We have all done that."

He was eating the *pâté* sandwiches as he spoke and drinking a glass of champagne.

Then he gazed at Zelda and sighed,

"I am sorry if I was angry and upset you before I left."

Zelda put up her hands.

"Oh, please don't or I will have to apologise to you again for all I said last night, Your Grace. I lay awake for a long time thinking how silly I had been."

The Duke smiled.

"In which case let's both of us start again from the beginning and forget last night and this morning. We must only remember that we have so much to discuss together and naturally argue about."

"I think now I am frightened of the arguments."

"Nonsense! I don't believe you are frightened of anything. It was very brave of you to tell me the truth."

Zelda gave a little cry.

"You are not to think about it. You are to forget it and we will start again, Your Grace."

"Very well. I think now it is nearly time to dress for dinner and I hope you will join me again. When we will enjoy, I hope, a very good meal and I want you to tell me about yourself and your family."

Zelda looked at him, then quickly turned away.

"As I would like a bath, I am going upstairs now to dress. I will think of several fascinating subjects we can argue about at dinner!"

She left the room before the Duke could open the door for her.

He thought, as he watched her move quickly down the passage, that her figure was certainly that of a young girl and not of an older woman.

'I was so gullible,' he told himself, 'to be deceived by her. Equally her make-up is exceedingly clever. It never struck me for a moment that she was wearing a wig or that those large spectacles were not necessary.'

He had been so intent during the day in coping with the farm fire that he had not thought about Zelda.

Now she was nagging away again in his mind.

He thought as he went upstairs a little later that it was in fact the most intriguing puzzle he had ever been presented with.

It was ridiculous to think that she might be trying to steal his possessions, but, if that was not the reason for her being at Minster Abbey, why had she come?

The Duke turned it over and over in his mind all the time he was having his bath and changing for dinner.

Harber had asked him if it could be at eight o'clock as the cook had sent to the village for certain items she needed and that had taken time.

"Are we in the small dining room or the big one?" the Duke asked Harber when he was finally dressed.

"The big one, Your Grace, and I've put on the table the special orchids you brought back from Nepal."

"Are they in bloom?" the Duke exclaimed. "That's splendid."

He felt, as he walked downstairs, it was something that would interest and please Mrs. König.

After all, few people visited Nepal and it would be a new place for her to hear about.

He had not been very long in the sitting room when Zelda joined him.

Tonight she had hesitated as to whether she should wear another of Lady Craven's black dresses or one of her own, but she wanted the Duke to see her looking her best despite her wig and glasses.

So she put on a gown she had bought for herself and which she particularly liked.

It was white, as she thought at her pretended age it would be correct for her to wear.

It had been designed by the great Frederick Worth, whose dress designs had made Paris the smartest and most fashionable City in the world.

Like all Worth's gowns it was elaborate and the soft muslin in which the gown was made was decorated with lace and flowers and it glittered when she moved with hidden diamante.

It was, as Zelda realised only too well, a gown for a ball rather than a quiet evening, but she so wanted, despite her disguise, the Duke to see her looking her very best.

She knew that the way the gown clung to her figure revealed her tiny waist and it was indeed a perfect frame for her beautiful figure.

The Duke, because he had seen her asleep, knew far better than Zelda how lovely she really was.

When she entered the room, it was with the greatest difficulty he prevented himself from asking her to take off her wig and throw away her large spectacles.

They went into dinner.

Even before he pointed them out to her, Zelda saw the orchids and exclaimed at their beauty.

Then she sat enthralled as the Duke told her of his visit to Nepal and how he had not only brought back the orchids but ancient manuscripts from a famous Monastery.

He was doing all the talking and Zelda listened to him enchanted and fascinated by all he had to say.

The food was even more delicious than it had been the night before and the menu more elaborate.

"I can see that the cook has responded well to your appreciation of her cooking, Mrs. König. She will be very disappointed if we don't eat every dish she provides."

"You must be very hungry, Your Grace. She has already given me a large luncheon and there was a cake for tea that was quite different from any I have tried before, and made me, I confess, unusually greedy."

The Duke laughed.

"Well, if we continue to eat at this rate, we will both be very fat in a month's time!

Zelda felt her heart leap.

He was talking about her staying for a month.

This meant that he did not intend to get rid of her immediately and her fear that this was the last meal they would have together was no longer lurking behind what she had to say.

They laughed and talked until finally Harber and the footman left them.

The Duke had a liqueur in front of him while Zelda was still sipping her coffee.

"I really don't think," he said, "I have ever enjoyed a meal more."

"I was thinking the same, Your Grace, but please tell me more about Nepal. I am absolutely fascinated by your description of the country and its people. You must write it all in a book."

"I think it would make a very good chapter."

"Of course it would," she agreed. "So would all the other places you have been to. It would thrill people who have not been as lucky as you have."

"You will have to help me with it," the Duke said. "And I think we should start by making a list of all the places I have been that you think would interest the readers who are not able to travel in the same way I have."

"We will, Your Grace, but we must not, while we are doing so, forget your amazing library."

"Of course not," he replied.

They moved into the drawing room.

But Zelda realised that, as he had been on his feet all day coping with the fire, he was tired.

"What I am going to do," she said, "is to send you to bed just as your mother would have done if she had been here. You have had a long day and I expect you will have to go out early tomorrow to see if anything untoward has happened during the night."

There was a soft gentle note in her voice.

It made the Duke feel almost as if his mother was indeed speaking to him.

At the same time he was very conscious of how beautiful she was when he could see her hair and her face.

He so wanted to tell her to wipe away the lines she had drawn under her eyes and at the corners of her mouth.

But he knew she was right and he really was very tired and there would be plenty of evenings ahead when they could talk even more than they had tonight.

Sooner or later he would undoubtedly tell her that he knew she was in disguise and then he could appreciate her loveliness.

"Very well," he said aloud. "I will do what you say. But tomorrow, if I ride over to the farm, I think you should come with me."

Zelda drew in her breath and stared at him.

"Do you really mean that, Your Grace?"

"I am quite certain you ride extremely well and my horses don't get enough exercise."

"I have been longing to ride ever since I saw you on that magnificent horse you were riding yesterday," Zelda added excitedly.

"That is Silver Sword. Tomorrow it would be a good idea if you rode him yourself. I have his twin to ride and I know they will enjoy what they have never been able to do – going out together!"

Zelda clasped her hands together.

"Thank you, thank you, Your Grace!" she enthused. "I will not sleep tonight. Tomorrow must come quickly because it will be so exciting."

"Very well, Mrs. König, but now, because we are very good children when we want to be, we will both go to bed."

They walked up the stairs together.

When they reached Zelda's room, she said,

"Thank you again, Your Grace, and I only hope the night will pass quickly before I go with you to the stables at – ?"

She waited for him to say the time and the Duke replied,

"As we have a long distance to go and will not be able to return in time for breakfast, I suggest we leave after we have had the first meal of the day, say at ten o'clock."

"That will most certainly suit me. Goodnight, Your Grace, and thank you again."

She went into her bedroom, closing the door behind her and then, pulling off her wig, she ran to the dressing table to put it down and to look at herself in the mirror.

'How is it possible,' she asked herself, 'that he is being so kind to me? Perhaps after we have been to the farm tomorrow, I can tell him why I am here.'

Then she was almost afraid to do so in case it made him angry again and he was not as kind to her as he was being at this moment.

'I must be careful, very careful,' she decided.

Because she was so excited at what lay ahead, she undressed quickly.

Then she brushed her golden hair as her mother had told her to do until it seemed almost to dance round the room in the candlelight.

She climbed into her bed and blew out the candles beside her.

Almost immediately she fell asleep.

*

Then unexpectedly she woke up.

She had the feeling that someone had called her, but when she listened there was no sound in the darkness.

'I must have dreamt it,' she told herself.

Then she felt as if the room was rather airless and perhaps she had not opened the window enough before she had climbed into bed.

She slipped out and walked with bare feet over the thick carpet to the window.

When she pulled back the curtains, she saw that the moonlight was as brilliant as it had been the night before and it was throwing a silver light over the garden.

She opened the window wide, not only to breathe in the fresh air but also to have a glimpse of the fountain with its water still flung up into the sky.

Then she looked towards the woods beyond the garden and they too seemed to catch the moonlight and many of the leaves appeared silver.

There was no wind and the trees were very still.

There seemed to be a hush over everything.

Then suddenly she became aware of a movement.

It was at the far end of the garden heading towards the house.

She thought at first it must be an animal, perhaps a horse that had escaped from the paddock.

Then she was certain that something was moving through the trees higher than a horse's head would be.

Whatever it was, it was coming straight towards the house and she leant out of the window trying to see what it could be.

Then suddenly as it came nearer she realised that it was a ladder, a very long one, that appeared to be moving of its own freewill above the bushes.

Zelda then stared at it coming slowly, silently and relentlessly forward.

She realised it must be carried by two men and she could guess why they were coming.

With a murmur of horror she turned away from the window and pulled open the door into the boudoir.

She ran across it, just as she was in her nightgown and then opened the boudoir door into the corridor.

She ran along it as quickly as she could towards the Master suite at the far end.

She dashed in.

The Duke had pulled back his curtains before he went to bed and the moonlight showed Zelda where he was sleeping in a huge four-poster draped with velvet curtains.

Without thinking of herself or her appearance, she flung herself against him screaming,

"Wake up! Wake up!"

The Duke opened his eyes.

"Please wake up!" Zelda repeated. "There are men coming to rob you and they are going to enter the house by the roof!"

The Duke, who was staring at her, was suddenly alert.

"By the roof!" he exclaimed. "We did not think of that."

"Look out – and you will see them."

The Duke sprang out of bed, picking up as he did so, a long dark blue robe.

He pulled it on as he ran to the window.

Then, when he looked out he could see approaching the house on his right where the library was situated, was the end of a very long ladder.

As he turned from the window, he found that Zelda was beside him.

"What can we do," she murmured.

"Look in the top drawer of that chest over there," he urged, "while I put on some clothes."

Zelda went to where he pointed and pulled open the drawer.

There were quite a number of objects in it and it took her a moment or two to find there were two revolvers in one corner with some bullets beside them.

On the other side of the drawer there were several daggers and stilettos that the Duke must have collected on his travels.

She could hear the Duke opening the wardrobe and moving behind her and so kept her back to him and then she loaded the two revolvers without any difficulty.

A moment later he joined her.

She saw he was wearing a shirt with an open neck, long trousers and slippers.

"So you found them, Mrs. König?"

"I have just loaded them, Your Grace."

"Then we will now go up onto the roof. Here is something for you to put over your nightgown."

He pulled over her shoulders a silk dressing gown, which she could fasten round her waist with the sash. This she did and then turned back the cuffs so that the sleeves were the right length for her.

While she was doing this, the Duke was inspecting the revolver and putting more bullets into the pockets of his trousers.

Then he asked her,

"I see you have loaded two revolvers. Can you shoot?"

"Very accurately," Zelda replied.

"Then come on."

He led the way across the room and when they reached the corridor, he turned to the left.

Although Zelda thought that the Master suite was at the end, there was a small passage leading to another door.

Before the Duke opened it, Zelda was aware that it was one of the heavy doors in front of the stairs that led up to the roof.

The Duke went ahead.

The steps, which were of stone, spiralled upwards.

Following behind him Zelda guessed that at the top there would be another door opening onto the roof itself.

It was, as she now realised, just directly above the library, which was at the far end of that part of the house.

When the Duke opened the door, he first looked out carefully onto the roof ahead.

Then bending low so that he could not be seen, he moved forward until he was kneeling against the parapet and bending too to make herself smaller, Zelda followed him.

They were now both kneeling on the left side of the roof.

There were sounds below them that told Zelda the men were laying the long ladder against the wall.

She drew in her breath.

Then, as if now he was sure that the men were just below him, the Duke bent over the parapet and fired a shot from his revolver.

The explosion seemed tremendous and it echoed in the air.

There was a shriek of alarm at being shot at from the men below.

The Duke fired again, not aiming at anything, but making the air ring with the sound.

"That should frighten those devils away," he said, speaking for the first time since they had left his bedroom.

Zelda was about to reply when there was another sound from behind them.

She turned round and saw to her horror the head and shoulders of another man rising on the other side of the roof.

She had never thought for a single moment that there might be more than one ladder.

The man on it was just about to climb onto the roof behind them.

And there was a revolver in his hand and he was pointing it at the Duke!

Without hesitating, Zelda aimed her revolver at him and pulled the trigger.

As she shot him in the shoulder, the man then fell backwards and screamed as he crashed onto the ground below.

It was then that the other men lost their nerve.

They abandoned their ladders and started to run as fast as they could back through the trees, shouting at one another to follow.

Now their voices grew fainter and fainter and soon neither the Duke nor Zelda could hear them anymore.

As she gave a sigh of relief, the Duke turned round and put his arms round her.

"You saved my life as well as my possessions," he breathed, "and I am very grateful to you."

He pulled her close to him.

Before she realised what was happening, his lips were on hers.

He kissed her and she felt a sudden ecstasy running through her body that she had never known before.

The Duke raised his head.

"I never thought this would happen," he muttered, "or that I would kiss you in such peculiar and unexpected circumstances."

"I think I wounded – that man," Zelda managed to mumble.

"We will see to him later. At the moment I am just thinking that you are even lovelier than when I first saw you and I never knew that anything could be as wonderful as your lips."

"But how – when – ?" she stammered.

"I will explain it all later," the Duke interrupted and kissed her again.

He could see her glorious golden hair shining in the moonlight and her piercing blue eyes staring at him and knew he had made no mistake when he had seen her asleep in her bed that morning.

Then, as he guided her towards the door they had climbed onto the roof through, she exclaimed shakily,

"What can we do? What will happen to all those men?"

"I will notify the Police, but I doubt if they will ever catch them," the Duke replied. "But first we must go down and tell the staff to see to the man who is wounded, if not dead."

"He was – pointing his pistol at you – "

"And you saved me," the Duke said quietly. "But let us talk about it in more comfortable circumstances than these."

He helped her to the door and was aware that she was wearing nothing on her feet.

"You have been very brave and wonderful," he said. "So wonderful that I have so much to tell you and I feel that you have a good deal to tell me."

Zelda gave a little laugh because she could not help herself.

"I am sure this is all a dream and it cannot really be happening."

"But it is," the Duke insisted, "and I want to now go where I can kiss you properly and tell you how lovely and amazing you are, my darling."

Zelda felt completely bewildered, not only by what was happening but by all that the Duke was saying to her.

However, it was impossible to say anything more as they descended the spiral stairs.

When they reached the bottom, the Duke's valet and Harber were running down the corridor towards them.

"We hears shots, Your Grace," Harber called out breathlessly.

"I know. There were some men intending to steal my treasures from the library. We were foolish, Harber, that, when we strengthened the windows, we did not think of anyone coming in through the roof."

"No we didn't, Your Grace. I thinks it'd be too high for them to reach it."

"But they did reach it. And, as one of them is lying wounded on the grass, you had both better go and see to him. If he is alive, he must be handed over to the Police."

"Very good, Your Grace."

There were expressions of excitement on Harber's face and the valet's.

It made Zelda realise that they were both thrilled by something new happening, even though it might have been a serious burglary.

They looked at her in amazement, but did not say anything.

"Now hurry as quickly as you can and then come and report to me whether the man is alive or dead. We will be in Mrs. König's boudoir."

"Very good, Your Grace," Harber said and the two men ran off the way they had come.

The Duke opened the door into her boudoir.

As soon as they were inside, he took Zelda into his arms and kissed her again.

There was only the light of the full moon coming through on either side of the curtains.

Zelda still could not believe what was happening to her, but she felt her whole body respond to the Duke's ardent kisses.

As he pulled her closer, she thought that she had never known anything so perfect as his lips.

"Now I want to know," he asked in a deep voice, "what you feel about me."

"I love you," Zelda murmured, "but I did not know it was love until you kissed me. It is so completely and utterly wonderful – it can only be love."

"That is exactly what it is," the Duke replied, "and I have been in love with you, my darling, since I went into your bedroom to give you the newspaper."

She made a little sound of surprise, but he went on,

"I saw sleeping in your bed, not the middle-aged librarian I had engaged, but a beautiful, adorable young angel, who must have dropped down from Heaven itself!"

Zelda laughed.

"I never thought of you coming into my bedroom," she confessed.

"Go now and put on a warm dressing gown, my precious," the Duke said, "while I light an oil lamp. Or do you prefer candles?"

"I think the candles would be more romantic at this moment," Zelda mumbled.

She slipped into her bedroom and put on the pretty negligee she had bought in Paris and the slippers to match.

She took one look in the mirror at her golden hair falling over her face.

Then, because she wanted so much to be with the Duke, she ran back into the boudoir.

He had already lit the candles and the room was looking very lovely, but she had eyes only for him and he was looking so tall and handsome.

He was gazing at her with an expression on his face she had not seen before.

With a superhuman effort she managed to walk slowly towards him.

Only as she reached him, did he put out his arms and once again his lips found hers and she was flying to the stars.

He kissed her until they were both breathless and then he pulled her down onto the sofa beside him.

"I love you, my darling, and this has been a Fairy story from the first moment you walked into the house. I think I knew then there was something about you I could not lose, but now I have found you I will never let you go."

With a smile on his lips, he added,

"In fact you are a prisoner here from now on and you can never escape."

"Are you really saying this to me?" Zelda asked in a small voice.

She knew she must be dreaming.

"I am not only saying it to you," the Duke averred, "but we are going to be married as soon as you tell me who you are and why you are here in my house. If you want to, we will travel to Nepal for our honeymoon. It seems a suitable place after all we said about it tonight."

"How can you think of anything so wonderful and so perfect?" Zelda asked. "I never thought, I only dreamt that when I came to England that I would find someone I not only loved – but who wanted to marry me for myself."

"Why should anyone want to marry you for any other reason?" the Duke enquired.

Then before she could reply, he laughed.

"I suppose, just as you are not an elderly woman, your name is not Giana König?"

She turned her face against his neck and whispered,

"Please don't be shocked, but my name is Princess Zelda of Brienz."

She felt the Duke stiffen as she added quickly,

"Please say you don't mind."

"Of course I don't mind. And I would marry you whoever you are or wherever you came from. I am just surprised. Why on earth, if you are a Princess, are you here in my house pretending to be an elderly librarian?"

"It does sound funny when you say it like that," Zelda answered. "But I really came here to see if I was a relation of yours."

"Relation!" the Duke exclaimed.

"It has always been a scandal in my family. My father had an accident and the doctors said he would never father any children," Zelda related in a small voice. "But your cousin, the fourth Duke, before he inherited, came to stay with my father and mother and nine months afterwards I was born."

He gave such a sudden cry that she was startled.

"Now I know who you remind me of. It has been puzzling me ever since I saw you without that ridiculous wig and those horrible spectacles. I want to show it to you now, but it will keep until tomorrow."

"Show me what?" Zelda enquired.

"A picture of your grandmother, as I now know her to be. I kept thinking after I had seen you asleep yesterday morning, or was it this morning, that you reminded me of someone I knew although I could not think who it was."

He paused for a moment to reflect and then added,

"But of course there is a delightful portrait of your grandmother, painted in Italy by one of the great artists. It is hanging in the bedroom which she always used when she came here."

"Oh, then I really am your relation," Zelda cried. "It makes me so proud to think that your blood flows in my veins."

"That is what I want you to feel, Zelda, and now I understand why you know so much about Scotland. Your grandmother was the daughter of the Duke of Sutherland, and was very proud of it, just as I am very proud that you will belong to me."

"And I am thrilled to belong to you. I ran away because Papa wanted me to marry some horrible King from the Balkans."

"Why should he want that?" the Duke asked.

"Because it would enhance our family's standing in Switzerland. Since it became a Republic, we are of very little importance."

"You will be very important to me, Zelda. In fact so important that I will do exactly as you want me to do and even take my place as I should have done at Windsor Castle."

He kissed her forehead before he added,

"I don't intend to spend very much time with Her Majesty when I might be with you."

"I will be jealous if you do," Zelda whispered.

She put her arms round his neck and sighed,

"This is so wonderful and so marvellous. We have found each other and we will be divinely happy because I am yours and you are mine. No one can ever separate us."

The Duke kissed her.

"Of course I do realise now that I ought to share my possessions with people who admire them. But the one thing I am not going to share, my beautiful one, is *you*. I will be a very jealous husband, and if any man tries to flirt with you, I will shoot him, as you shot the ruffian who might have killed me."

"Don't talk about it. It frightens me," Zelda sighed.

The door then opened and Harber came in.

She moved out of the Duke's arms, but they were still close together on the sofa.

"We've found that burglar, Your Grace," Harber announced with a grin.

He was obviously very pleased with himself.

"Is he dead?" the Duke asked.

"No, Your Grace, only wounded in the shoulder and badly bruised from falling such a long way. But he fell in a flowerbed so I don't think any bones be broken."

"What have you done with him?

"We woke up the grooms, Your Grace, and they be taking him to the Police Station. The doctor can attend to him there and the Police'll be coming up to see Your Grace in the morning."

"That's splendid, Harber," the Duke said. "Thank you for all you have done and I am very grateful. Tell the gardener to remove the ladders that are lying up against the house and lock them up."

"I'll do that, Your Grace," Harber replied. "And be there anything you be wanting at this moment?"

"I was thinking that we might celebrate our victory over the robbers with a glass of champagne. I think you will enjoy one too, Harber."

"That's real kind of Your Grace. I'll bring a bottle up in the ice-bucket straight away."

He left the room and the Duke laughed.

"So you see, my darling, there will be no trouble. The man is not dead and everything is working out exactly as we want it to do."

"All I want," Zelda breathed, "is to be with you."

"That is exactly what you are going to be. We will be married at once in my Chapel and then go away on our honeymoon. Only when we come back will we tell people what has happened."

"I cannot do that," Zelda said. "I have to tell Papa and Mama or they will be very hurt and of course Lady Craven who I was staying in London with."

"Lady Craven? I remember her."

"And she remembers you well. We will have to tell them what we are doing."

"We will tell them after we have done it," the Duke persisted. "I could not bear another wedding with my relations chattering about me at last doing my duty to the family."

"No, of course not," Zelda agreed. "We will get married as soon as you like and then we will just tell Lady

Craven who has been so kind. Next we will go home and tell Papa and Mama that we are married and of course my Cousin Johann."

"Were you really his librarian, Zelda?"

"Not officially, but he has always let me read all the books in his library, which really is fantastic."

"So are you. We will do exactly what you want, my darling, but I have to have you alone with me. If we start our honeymoon in Switzerland, we can easily go from there to anywhere in the world you wish as long as we are together."

"We will do that," Zelda said, "and when we come back, you have already promised me that you will prove yourself to be the most intelligent, clever and influential man in the whole country."

"I knew marriage would do this to me," the Duke sighed. "But because I want to please you and because I love you and because you are the most perfect woman I have ever imagined, I will do exactly as you say."

"Before we leave," Zelda suggested, "we must have the roof of the library made much stronger than it is at the moment and also protect it from below."

The Duke laughed.

"That is just what I love about you. You are so practical, so amazingly sensible and at the same time so utterly adorable."

Then he was kissing her again.

Kissing her until it was just impossible for them to think of anything except themselves.

Both of them in their own way had found love.

The love that all men and women seek but very few are clever or lucky enough to find, the love that comes from God and is, for those who find it, Heaven itself.